JESS THE BORDER COLLIE
The Gift

'What's up, Dad?' Matt asked, sitting on the edge of the bed.

Jenny sat beside him, rubbing her eyes. 'I'm so sleepy, Dad . . . I don't think . . .'

'This won't take a minute,' Jenny's father spoke hurriedly. He looked flustered and uncomfortable. 'I just wanted to know how . . . you would feel . . . if I asked Ellen to marry me?'

Jenny's heavy eyelids flew wide open and she gasped. An unexpected feeling of joy surged through her and she leaped off the bed and ran to hug her father. 'Yes!' she said. 'Oh, yes! It feels . . . *right*. It *is* right. Yes!'

The GIFT

LUCY DANIELS

Hodder
Children's
Books

a division of Hodder Headline

With special thanks to Ingrid Hoare

Text copyright © 2000 Working Partners Ltd
Created by Working Partners Ltd, 1 Albion Place, London W6 0QT
Illustrations copyright © 2000 Sheila Ratcliffe
Jess the Border Collie is a trademark of
Working Partners Limited

First published in Great Britain in 2000
by Hodder Children's Books

A Catalogue record for this book is available from the British Library

ISBN 0 340 77848 2

Typeset by Avon Dataset Ltd, Bidford-on-Avon, Warks

Printed and bound in Great Britain by
The Guernsey Press Co. Ltd, Channel Isles

Hodder Children's Books
a division of Hodder Headline
338 Euston Road
London NW1 3BH

1

'What's this?' Jenny Miles glanced down at her feet, then into the warm brown eyes of Jess, her Border collie. 'It's a toy, Jess. Who does it belong to?'

Jenny looked around, but she and her dog were alone in the fields above Cliffbay. Her sweeping gaze took in the distant, red rooftops of Windy Hill, the sheep farm where she lived in the village of Graston.

Jess dropped the toy on Jenny's shoe. It was the battered remains of a doll. Then the collie took it gently into his mouth, tossed it aside and pounced on it with both front paws.

'Oh, I know!' Jenny laughed. 'I forgot to bring your *ball*, is that it?' She ruffled the sleek fur on his head, then picked up the toy and threw it – overarm – with all her might. Jess raced after it, barking happily.

Jenny grinned at him. *I should have remembered your ball*, she thought, feeling guilty. She had been so wrapped up in thinking about Carrie, she had overlooked the fun Jess often had on his walks with a tennis ball. Her thoughts switched again to her friend.

Jenny had recently found out that Carrie Turner had leukaemia – a type of cancer that was affecting her blood. She and Jenny had been best friends since one day at school when Carrie, her green eyes ablaze, had taken Jenny's side in an argument with Fiona MacLay. Jenny hadn't dared to hope that the new girl, a bubbly and confident redhead, would want her as a friend. She could hardly believe it when Carrie had invited her out on a day trip to Puffin Island. Their friendship had gone from strength to strength. Now Carrie was facing a frighteningly uncertain future, and Jenny was trying to do everything she could to help her.

Jenny looked over at Jess. The collie had given up trying to make the doll bounce and had decided to roll on it instead. He yelped with pleasure as he wiggled about on his back, all four of his white feet up in the air. Jenny burst out laughing.

'First sign of madness, laughing at nothing, all on your own.'

Jenny started and looked behind her. 'Oh!' she said. 'You scared me, David.'

David Fergusson grinned and stooped to let his Border collie, Orla, off her lead. 'Sorry! Have I missed something funny?' he asked, pushing his curly dark hair away from his eyes.

'I was laughing at Jess,' said Jenny, watching Orla bound towards her playmate.

David and his father had moved recently to Cliffbay, and David had joined Greybridge Senior, Jenny's school. He was a secretive boy, and hard to get to know, but Jenny liked him as much as Jess liked Orla.

David's face suddenly clouded. 'How's Carrie?' he asked. 'She's missing quite a bit of her schoolwork, isn't she?'

'I don't think she's feeling well enough to worry about school,' Jenny said gravely. 'But she's cheerful and full of hope,' she added brightly. 'Did you know she's found someone who is going to donate their bone marrow to her?'

David wrinkled his nose. 'Yes,' he said, 'but I'm not exactly sure what that means.'

'It's called a transplant,' Jenny explained, walking in step with David behind the dogs. 'The doctor can put healthy blood into Carrie's sick blood to try and make her better. Only, the blood they put into her has to be *exactly* the same type as her own, or her body will reject it.'

'I see . . . I think . . . but what exactly is *marrow*?' David looked puzzled.

'Bone marrow is the tissue which makes the blood cells,' Jenny said knowledgeably, adding: 'Carrie's explained it all to me.'

'When will she have this . . . transplant?' David asked.

'First, she has to have very high doses of a drug, a treatment called chemotherapy,' Jenny said. 'It's to destroy the sick bone marrow and make way for the new, healthy marrow. But it's not very pleasant and it makes Carrie feel sick.'

'Poor Carrie,' David muttered sympathetically. He picked up a stick and hurled it, sending it flying. Orla sprinted after it. Jenny's eyes followed its path and she saw Fiona MacLay strolling towards them.

Fiona waved. Her younger brother Paul was racing along with his Border terrier puppy, Toby, who was snapping playfully at his ankles.

'Hello,' Jenny called.

Jess had disentangled himself from his game with Orla and the two dogs hurried over to sniff Toby in greeting. Jess and Orla's tails swept from side to side in welcome, while Toby's compact little body shuddered with excitement. His stump of a tail wiggled happily.

Fiona came over to Jenny and David. 'Have you heard?' she began, her eyes wide. 'Carrie's going to have an operation to make her better . . . that lady from the SSPCA centre is going to give Carrie some of the marrow from inside her bones!'

'Yes, we know,' David said, as though he had known for ages.

'Sarah Taylor came up to Windy Hill to tell us,' Jenny said, her eyes shining. 'She's so kind – as well as brave!' she added. There had been a bleak and frightening period when it had looked as though no suitable match for Carrie's marrow would be found. Then they had met Sarah.

'Who *is* Sarah?' Paul asked. 'Do I know her?' The little boy was out of breath from his race with Toby.

'I don't think so,' Jenny said. 'She works at the

wildlife hospital. She met Carrie when we took those oil-covered birds from Puffin Island there for help. Remember?'

But Paul had lost interest and wandered away to find a stick for Toby.

David found a stone, and lobbed it at the trunk of a nearby tree. 'Bullseye!' he said.

'Carrie's not feeling well at all,' Fiona stated glumly. 'I wish we could do something to cheer her up.'

'Me too,' Jenny said. She watched the three dogs playing.

Jess was leading Orla in a merry game around the field. He streaked through the grass, leaping effortlessly over anything in his way. Orla was close on his heels, her pink tongue lolling. Toby was lost from view, swallowed up by the tall spring grasses, as he bobbed gamely along behind.

It gave Jenny an idea. 'I know what we could do!' she said suddenly. Fiona and David turned to her and even Paul looked up, alerted by the excitement in her voice. Jenny paused until she was certain that she had the full attention of her companions. 'Let's organise a sponsored walk!'

'A *what*?' said David.

'What for?' Fiona asked, frowning.

'A sponsored walk . . . to show Carrie how much

we care!' Jenny said triumphantly. 'We'll get all of Graston – and Cliffbay too – out walking – for miles! There'll be a prize at the end of it . . . and we'll ask everyone to give the money they raise to cancer research, or something.'

'Hey,' Fiona said slowly. 'That's not a bad idea. Carrie would know then that the whole village is thinking about her.'

'It sounds as if it might be a bit far. Will Toby make it?' Paul asked, looking doubtfully at Toby's short legs.

'I'm sure he will.' Jenny smiled.

'We'll have to plan a route first, then let everyone know. We could put up a poster at school,' Fiona suggested.

'We've got a computer at home, with a new colour printer. My dad's got plenty of free time because he doesn't work . . . well, not at the moment, anyway. I'm sure he'll help us.' David sounded enthusiastic. But suddenly he frowned and looked searchingly at Jenny. 'Doesn't Carrie mind everyone knowing that she's ill?'

'She did in the beginning,' Jenny said. 'But she's fine with it now. She thinks it's easier to tell people. Just imagine what might have happened if I hadn't told Sarah about her leukaemia! She might still be looking for the right person to give her their bone marrow.'

'You're right.' Fiona shuddered. 'Oh, poor Carrie! Let's go home and talk about our plans for this sponsored walk straightaway, shall we?'

'Let's go to my house,' David said, taking Orla's lead from round his neck. 'We'll go there first and ask my dad if we can use the computer.'

Jenny nodded and smiled. She felt her spirits rise. At last she would be doing something positive to support her friend. Keeping busy would make the waiting for Carrie's transplant, and its result, so much easier.

Jess trotted over and sat down at Jenny's feet. He put his head to one side. His sides were heaving with the effort of his energetic play with Orla and Toby. He held up a dirty white paw and Jenny took it gently. 'Yes,' she murmured. 'You can take part too. Jenny and Jess Miles – we'll make a great team.'

'Come on!' David had gone on ahead. 'Let's get moving.'

The wind began to tug at Jenny's fair, shoulder-length hair as she walked with her friends across the field. The farm she lived on, with her father, Fraser Miles, and their housekeeper and friend Ellen Grace, had been perfectly named. It *was* on a windy hill, and it was the place that Jenny loved best in the world.

The sloping acres, that were given over to the blackface sheep Fraser Miles farmed, had originally belonged to Jenny's mother's family. When Sheena Miles had died tragically and suddenly, Jenny's dad had been more determined than ever that Windy Hill would survive, not only as a thriving business – but as a happy home for Jenny and her brother Matt.

'Is Matt coming back this weekend?' Fiona asked, cutting into Jenny's thoughts.

'Yep, he should be,' Jenny replied happily. Nineteen-year-old Matt was away studying at agricultural college, but he liked to spend his weekends at home on the farm. Jenny was always pleased to see him. 'No doubt Mrs Grace is getting ready for Matt by spending today cooking a mountain of food.' She giggled.

It hadn't been easy to accept the idea of Ellen Grace coming to live at Windy Hill. At first, it had seemed to Jenny that, somehow, her mother was being replaced. But over the past couple of years, Mrs Grace's wise and gentle presence had made her a valued member of the family.

Jess trotted along, obediently keeping pace with

Jenny's heel. Fiona and Paul took turns holding Toby on his lead.

'Here we are,' said David, when they reached the small white bungalow he shared with his father. The neat little garden was surrounded by a picket fence. As David swung open the gate, Orla slipped past him and round a flowering bush, before making a protective dive for an old bone lying on the lawn. Her lead became entangled in a low-lying branch.

'Hang on!' scolded David irritably, stooping to untangle it. 'Jess isn't even interested in that smelly old bone. Neither is Toby.'

Jenny was first to follow David through the gate and she smiled at the sight of her friend, on his hands and knees, grappling to free Orla. She looked at the front door, painted a bright blue, and noticed a note pinned there. She stepped up to read it.

Douglas – I had to go out. Be back around 5.30. Dad.

'Douglas?' Jenny said. She turned to see David striding up the garden towards her. 'Who's Douglas?' she asked, wrinkling her nose.

David blushed. He reached round Jenny and quickly tore the note from the door. The drawing pin that secured it flew off and hit the stone step with a little pinging sound. Crumpling the paper in his hand David stuffed it into his jeans' pocket. 'It's . . . er . . . a name, a silly *pet* name that my father calls me. Nothing else.'

Jenny was taken aback by his defensiveness. 'That's fine,' she said quietly, as Fiona and Paul came through the gate. 'I was only wondering.'

'Is your dad at home?' Fiona asked.

'No,' David said, looking flustered. 'But it's best if I talk to him on my own, later. I'll let you know what he says.'

In the kitchen at Cliff House, Carrie was pouring Coke from a big plastic bottle. 'I'm glad you've come,' she said, grinning at Jenny and Fiona. 'Sundays can be so boring when you're stuck at home.'

'How are you feeling?' Fiona asked.

'Awful, most of the time.' Carrie made a face. 'It's the chemotherapy. But at least I don't have to worry about maths and geography and tests and . . .'

'Lucky you!' Fiona interrupted.

Jenny shot a glance at Carrie and saw that she hadn't minded Fiona telling her she was lucky. *But really*, Jenny thought, *Carrie is far from lucky.* She would much rather have to face a maths test, every day for the next six months, than have a single moment of Carrie's leukaemia.

She took a longer look at her friend. Against the vibrant yellow and green of Mrs Turner's cheerful kitchen, her face was chalky pale. The woollen beret on her head was set at a jaunty angle, letting a few remaining wisps of the flame-red hair – once Carrie's most striking feature – escape. She watched Carrie set out the glasses and rip open a big bag of crisps. There was a muddy yellow bruise on the back of her hand from the drug treatment she'd been having. Every time Jenny saw her friend she couldn't get over how brave she was.

'You're quiet,' said Carrie, peering into Jenny's face. Then she looked under the table at Jess. 'And so are you, for a change.' She darted out a hand to the collie's cold and quivering nose.

'Jess misses you,' Jenny smiled.

'I miss him, too,' she said. 'I miss going for walks. And you wouldn't believe it, but I even miss being at school.'

'Do you really?' Fiona said, amazed. 'Seriously?'

'Seriously.' Carrie smiled at her friends. 'How's David?'

'Weird,' said Fiona immediately.

'Weird?' Carrie raised her eyebrows at Jenny.

'Tell her what happened yesterday, Jenny,' Fiona prompted.

'It was nothing, really,' Jenny said, sipping her drink. 'It was just . . . strange.'

'Strange how?' Carrie demanded, holding out her hand for Jess to lick her salty fingers.

'Yesterday morning, we were out walking and decided to go back to his house. Anyway, I got there first, with Jess, and I found a note pinned on the door . . .'

'It was to *Douglas* – from Dad!' Fiona squeaked.

'David said it was a pet name his father had for him. Douglas, I mean. But he went all red and cross because I'd seen the note before he did,' Jenny explained.

'Let's call him Douggie, then – if we want to tease him.' Carrie giggled.

'No, don't,' Jenny said gently. 'He seemed really upset about it. I don't know why.'

'It's a silly nickname for someone called David,' Fiona said. 'Dave or Davey would make more sense.'

'Maybe he was christened Douglas but his family

have always called him David,' Jenny suggested. 'You know, some people are called by their second names.'

'Ah, but maybe,' said Carrie, speaking in an eerie whisper, 'the Fergussons are not who they say they are. Maybe they're a couple of criminals, on the run from the police!' Her eyes narrowed in playful suspicion.

'Don't make up scary stories,' Jenny pleaded, laughing. 'I'm sure it's just a name from when he was younger that he doesn't like any more.'

'Well, I agree with Carrie,' Fiona said. 'I'm sure there's something funny going on in that bungalow.'

'What were you doing at his house, anyway?' Carrie asked.

'It all began with Jenny's brilliant idea,' Fiona said.

'Well, *I* think it's a brilliant idea. You might not!' Jenny smiled, but before she could go on, the door to the kitchen opened and Mrs Turner came in. She was holding a plastic laundry basket of newly-ironed clothes. A warm, lemony smell came into the room with her.

'All right, Carrie love?' she asked anxiously. Carrie gave her mother the thumbs-up sign. 'Is she being a good hostess, girls?' Mrs Turner smiled at Jenny and Fiona. With her free hand she smoothed Jess's head, sticking out from under the table.

'Yes, thanks,' Jenny said, eyeing Mrs Turner's outfit discreetly. Carrie's mum was an artist and Jenny loved the clothes she wore. She wasn't afraid of vibrant colours and she always looked bright and interesting. Today she was wearing a calf-length dress of scarlet and lilac stripes. Her red hair was loosely tied back with a yellow ribbon.

'Did your brother make it back this weekend, Jenny?' Mrs Turner asked, as she began to make preparations for supper.

'Yes,' Jenny said happily. 'And Dad was especially glad to see him. We're really busy on the farm at the moment,' she explained. 'Matt came in from the fields very late last night, and went out early this morning, so I've hardly had a chance to see him yet.'

'I expect Matt will find time for you before he has to go back to college,' Mrs Turner said, taking some carrots over to the kitchen sink.

'What about this brilliant idea of yours, then?' Carrie tugged at Jenny's sleeve, changing the subject. 'Go on, don't keep me in suspense.'

'Oh, yes.' Jenny eased her foot out from under Jess. The collie had fallen asleep under the kitchen table, with his head cushioned on her shoe. 'Well,' she began, 'I thought it would be fun to organise a sponsored walk through Graston and on, down to

Cliffbay and back, in a loop.'

Carrie blinked at her. 'Why?' she said, resting her elbows on the table and propping her chin in her hands.

'To raise money for charity – a cancer charity, I mean. What do you think?' Jenny's eyes were bright.

'I think that's really sweet of you,' Carrie smiled. 'But I don't think anyone will go for it. Why would anyone want to trudge all that way just because of a horrible illness?'

'Because it will be great fun!' Fiona said enthusiastically.

'We could take Jess, and Orla,' said Jenny, trying to interest Carrie in her idea. 'There'd be prizes for the first people to reach the finish – and *think* how much money we could collect.'

'It's a wonderful idea,' Mrs Turner said softly, coming to stand behind Carrie's chair. She smiled warmly at Jenny. 'It *would* be fun to go walking on a beautiful spring day, and it is for a very good cause.'

'What cause?' Carrie asked, turning to look up at her mother.

'Well,' Mrs Turner said, 'Sarah Taylor told me that her sister Katie spent time in a little hospice near Greybridge. I think it would be great if we could

raise some money and give it to the people who run
the place.'

'What's a hospice?' Fiona asked.

'It's a home for people who are too ill to stay in
their own homes,' Mrs Turner explained.

'Oh,' said Fiona.

'That's a great idea!' Jenny said, thrilled.

'OK, then,' Carrie said, suddenly grinning at Jenny.
'Let's organise a sponsored walk. What do I have to
do?'

'Nothing,' Jenny smiled. 'Except help us to design
the poster. David's father's got a computer with a
printer, so we thought we'd print quite a few posters
and put them up around Graston. There are still a lot
of details to be sorted out.'

'That will give me something to think about,'
Carrie said.

'When are you coming back to school?' Fiona
asked, draining the last of her drink.

'I don't know,' Carrie replied. She rubbed her eyes.
'Mum says it depends how I feel.'

Mrs Turner glanced at her wristwatch. 'I think you
should rest now, Carrie,' she said softly.

'Oh! Yes.' Jenny stood up and Jess immediately
came out from under the table. His eyes were glazed
with sleep. He shook himself and yawned. She

smoothed the top of his head. 'We'll get going, then.'

'Thanks for coming,' Carrie said, as Mrs Turner walked with Jenny and Fiona to the front door. 'And say hello to "Douggie" for me!'

Jenny wagged a playful finger at her friend. '*Don't* call him Douggie!' she chided, then giggled.

Jenny and Fiona cycled up the hilly lane from Cliffbay to Graston. Jess loped along easily beside them. Jenny was always pleased to see the collie keep up so effortlessly. There had been a time when she had wondered if Jess would ever walk without a severe limp, let alone be as strong and sure-footed as he was now.

Jess had been the runt of a litter born to Fraser Miles's beloved sheepdog, Nell. Jenny had been heartbroken when her father had suggested that the newly-born puppy, whose tiny, twisted leg hung uselessly, be put to sleep. Some spark of determination that Jenny had seen in the puppy's pleading eyes had made her beg for his life. Her father had relented, in spite of his belief that there was no room for a non-working dog on a busy sheep farm. So Jess had stayed, hand-reared by Jenny, and when he was older and stronger, an operation had all but completely mended his damaged leg.

Jenny was lost in memories of Jess as an adorable puppy, when Fiona braked abruptly at a fork in the road. 'Bye, Jenny. See you tomorrow at school,' she said.

'Bye, Fi. Don't forget to think about the details of our walk, will you?'

'I won't.' Fiona put a hand out towards Jess. He looked up at her and wagged his tail gently. Then, she cycled away towards Dunraven, the neighbouring farm to Windy Hill.

Jenny's tummy rumbled with hunger as she headed home. She could already see the grey stone farmhouse sitting solidly among the undulating fields, facing a sweep of sea. A rocky mound rose up behind Windy Hill and, perched on its crest was the ancient ruined keep called Darktarn – Jenny's favourite place to go when she wanted to be alone with her thoughts. She would have liked to go up there now, and think about the walk, and Carrie, but she was too hungry.

She dismounted and began to wheel her bike up the unmade track to the farm's gate. In the paddock, adjacent to the small shearing barn, Matt's stallion, Mercury, was rubbing his glossy shoulder up against the trunk of a tree. He skittered when he heard the wheels of Jenny's bike crunching into the gravel. The big horse tossed his mane and threw back his head, whickering and snorting in welcome.

'Oh no,' warned Jenny, as Mercury cantered up to the fence and stretched his sleek nose towards her. 'I haven't anything for you. Not even a peppermint. Sorry.'

She cupped the palm of her hand round his velvet-soft muzzle and looked into the large, liquid eyes of the horse. Mercury's smooth lips opened and closed, making a soft snapping sound, as he searched hopefully for a small titbit. Jenny chuckled. 'Silly old boy.'

Two years ago, Jenny's mother Sheena had been killed riding Mercury. She had fallen and broken her neck. Fraser Miles, struggling with his shock and his grief, had immediately sold his wife's horse, and had hoped never to see the animal again. But many months later, Matt had come across Mercury at the livestock market in Greybridge. Knowing that Mercury's fate was to be shot if he wasn't bought that day, Matt had taken pity on his mother's beloved horse and brought him back to Windy Hill.

Rubbing the little white smudge between the horse's eyes, Jenny wondered how she could ever have been so angry with Matt for having rescued Mercury. The horse had suffered greatly away from

THE GIFT

Windy Hill. The once-proud stallion came home broken both in health and in spirit. It had taken months to rebuild his confidence and make him well again.

'It wasn't your fault,' she whispered to Mercury, kissing his warm cheek. 'I know that now. I'm sorry if I ever had any bad thoughts about you. Only, we miss Mum so much, you see . . .'

Jenny broke off. The face of her mother came up brightly in her mind, making her chest tighten and ache. Sometimes the pain of having lost her was so great that Jenny could hardly bear it.

She heard the porch door to the kitchen open. Jenny turned to see Ellen Grace come out onto the top step and put a hand up to her eyes to block out the glare from the sinking sun.

She spotted Jenny at the fence to Mercury's paddock and called over to her. 'Time to eat, Jenny,' she called. 'Are you hungry?'

Jenny felt the pang in her chest ease a little. Her voice rose on the wind. 'Yes,' she yelled. 'I'm starving. I'm coming!' She took up her bicycle and began to wheel it hurriedly towards the house. 'Come on, Jess.'

But Jess was already bounding up the track towards Mrs Grace, his tail wagging furiously.

3

As Jenny propped her bike against the wall of the shed, she looked up at the sky. All around her it was streaked with stripes of luminous pink and soft grey, and she saw a first small star that had popped out above the sea. It was a beautiful sight, and she could make out the gentle bleating of the ewes and their lambs in the barn as they began to settle for the night. Feeling contented, she kicked off her shoes in the porch and flung open the door to the kitchen.

Matt and her father were seated at the big pine

table under the window. Jess was standing on his back legs, his tail thumping noisily against the leg of a chair. His front paws were on Matt's lap. 'Hey! You crazy dog,' Matt was laughing. 'Your paws are filthy. Hello, Jen. Can't you control this animal?'

'Hi, everyone. Jess, down!' Jenny commanded and the collie looked round and obediently crawled under the table. 'He's only pleased to see you,' Jenny grinned. 'Me, too!'

Matt half-rose and leaned towards Jenny for a hug. 'Sorry, I haven't had a chance to spend much time with you. Some of us have to work, while certain little princesses I could name snooze away Sunday mornings undisturbed . . .' he teased.

'Not true!' said Jenny indignantly. 'I was up early working too – on my history assignment.'

Matt patted her on the head. 'I'm only joking!' he laughed.

'How's Carrie, lass?' Fraser Miles poured himself a glass of water from the jug.

'Quite cheerful, today,' Jenny said, pulling a chair up to the table.

'Have you washed those hands?' Mrs Grace asked, frowning.

Jenny looked at her palms. There were traces of dirt on them – from Mercury's coat, she guessed. She smiled at Ellen Grace and went over to the sink.

'Carrie hasn't got much of her lovely red hair left, except for a few strands, and she looks even thinner,' Jenny reported. 'But she's still her fun self!'

'I expect she's much more hopeful now that a transplant has been arranged,' Mr Miles said, making room on the table for a big earthenware casserole dish that Mrs Grace had brought from the oven.

'Oh, yes,' Matt put in. 'Dad told me about the operation. Has Carrie been given a date for it yet?'

'No,' Jenny said, sitting down. 'But I think it will be quite soon.'

Mrs Grace served each of them in turn. Steam from the delicious-looking meal curled into the air. The room was fragrant with the scent of baking apples and sweet pastry. Fraser Miles broke off a hunk of bread from a home-made loaf and raised his glass. 'Ellen,' he said, 'this is wonderful, as always. Thank you.'

Jenny giggled. It was unlike her father to be so formal. But Mrs Grace raised her own glass, and gave Jenny's father a shy, girlish smile. Jenny giggled again, and Matt nudged her with his foot under the table.

'Hey!' she glared at her brother and he frowned at her.

'Mmm, thanks Mrs Grace,' Matt said, smiling

warmly, ignoring Jenny. 'This is delicious.'

Jenny began to eat, and glanced furtively across the table at Ellen Grace. She wore a marine-blue blouse and skirt Jenny hadn't seen before, and a pair of tiny gold earrings. She couldn't remember the last time she had seen Mrs Grace wearing anything other than her practical little work pinafore, covering a T-shirt and old jeans. She looked positively radiant. Jenny wondered with a little stab of guilt if today was perhaps Mrs Grace's birthday. In her head, she began to calculate the date. 'September . . .' she said aloud, without thinking.

'What about it?' said Matt.

'That's when your birthday is, isn't it, Mrs Grace?' Jenny looked closely at her.

'Yes, love, it is,' she replied, surprised. 'Ages away. Why?'

Jenny shook her head. 'Oh, no reason,' she said. 'I was just checking.'

'More rice, Jenny?' Mrs Grace asked.

'Yes, please. Oh, I haven't told you about my brilliant idea!'

Jenny had suddenly remembered the sponsored walk. Her dad, Matt and Mrs Grace gave her their full attention. Jess ventured out from under the table, encouraged by the excited tone of her voice. He sat beside her chair, and rested his cheek against her thigh.

'Fiona, David and I, and Carrie, are going to organise a sponsored walk to raise money for the hospice where Sarah Taylor's sister stayed when she was sick with leukaemia,' Jenny explained.

'Really?' Fraser Miles looked up from his plate.

'Don't make it *too* strenuous,' Matt groaned.

'That's a lovely idea, Jenny.' Ellen Grace smiled. 'And Carrie's keen on it?'

'She thought it was a great idea – eventually. She couldn't see the point of it at first. But, really, I just want everyone to know about Carrie's illness, and about how brave and strong she's being . . . and the nicer and kinder people are to her, then the better it'll be for her!' Jenny finished her sentence in a rush of emotion. Her cheeks felt hot and her eyes were suddenly stinging. She looked down at Jess, and put a hand to his soft chest. He licked her arm with a warm, loving tongue.

Ellen Grace put her hand on Jenny's shoulder and rubbed it soothingly. Very quietly, she said: 'And how brave and strong *you're* being, love.'

'Have you worked out the details of this walk, Jen lass?' Mr Miles looked up. He had been mopping up the last of the gravy on his plate with a piece of bread.

'It's got to be ten kilometres, tops,' said Matt firmly. 'No more, or people won't go for it.'

'How much can we ask people to pay, Dad?' Jenny asked.

'You could ask for a minimum of ten pence a kilometre. But I think you'll find that most people will be willing to pay more.'

'I think you're right, Fraser,' said Mrs Grace. 'Especially as it sounds like fun, too.'

'We're going to design some posters and paste them up all round Graston. I'm sure loads of people will want to take part when they hear about Carrie, and—' Jenny broke off, startled by the sudden, shrill ringing of the telephone.

'Now, who can that be calling on a Sunday night?' Mrs Grace looked at her watch. She put her knife and fork together on her plate.

'I'll go, Ellen.' Fraser Miles got up from the table, smiling at her. He patted her arm affectionately as he squeezed between the wall and her chair. Jenny caught Matt's eye and he raised his eyebrows at her.

'We had twins lambs born last night, Jen,' Matt said, helping himself to some more vegetables.

'Ah! Good. How lovely. Are they both doing all right?'

'Yep, two strong little lads,' Matt grinned.

Fraser Miles voice carried from the hall where he was speaking. 'Mr Fergusson? Yes, hello! How can I help you?'

'Perhaps David has left his homework a bit late, and wants some help from you, Jenny?' Mrs Grace whispered. Jenny shrugged, and listened to what her father was saying.

'Well, I'm sure it wouldn't be a problem. Of course, I'd like to check with Mrs Grace, my . . . housekeeper. But I feel sure she won't have any objections. Would you hold on for just a minute, please?'

'What is it?' hissed Jenny, when her father put his head round the door to the kitchen. Jess blinked and pricked up his ears.

'It seems that Mr Fergusson has been called away suddenly, on urgent business. He can't leave the lad alone in the house and there's nowhere for him to go. Would you mind if he came and stayed here at Windy Hill for a while, Jenny? Ellen?'

'Oh!' Jenny was surprised.

'I wouldn't mind a bit. He can have Ian's old room!' Ellen seemed pleased.

'Jen? Do you mind?' Her father looked searchingly at her.

'No, I don't mind,' Jenny replied. She supposed it wouldn't be any different to having Mrs Grace's nephew, Ian, around the farm. He had spent quite a long time with them while his parents were setting up home in Canada, and it had been all right.

'That's settled then.' Fraser Miles grinned. 'I'll go and tell Mr Fergusson.' He went back into the hallway.

'What's David like?' Matt asked.

'David? Oh, he's a nice boy,' Mrs Grace said kindly, collecting up the empty plates. Jenny stood up to help her.

'Yes, he is nice,' she said.

'You can put him to work on the farm,' Matt suggested, grinning.

'Matt!' Jenny scolded. 'He's got schoolwork to do. Loads of it, like me.'

'David can stay with us, Mr Fergusson,' Jenny heard her dad say. 'No problem. Tomorrow? Yes, I'm sure that's fine. OK, then. No bother. Goodnight.'

'Would you like a piece of apple pie?' Mrs Grace smiled as Fraser Miles came back into the room.

'Hmmm, is that what I can smell, Ellen? My favourite! You're spoiling us.'

'Dad?' Jenny was frowning. 'Did Mr Fergusson say what business it was that had called him away?'

'I didn't ask him, Jenny,' her father replied. 'Why?'

'It's just that only yesterday David told me and Fiona that his father didn't have any work to do. He said that his father would be able to help us print out some posters on his computer for our sponsored walk.' Jenny was puzzled.

'Perhaps this is something that isn't really work at all,' Ellen Grace suggested, as she sliced into the crust of the pie. 'It might have to do with family, or something.'

'Maybe someone's died,' Matt said helpfully. 'And it's a funeral. He has to go.'

'That's silly,' Jenny said. 'Why wouldn't he just say so then? Why talk about urgent business?'

'It doesn't matter anyway,' Mr Miles said gently. 'It isn't any of our business where he has to go, or why. All I know is that he's very grateful we're letting David stay here at Windy Hill.'

'What does he do, this Mr Fergusson?' Matt asked. 'Is he a farmer?'

'No.' Jenny shook her head. 'He's not. I don't know what he does. A bit of this and a bit of that, David says.'

'Odd,' said Matt, and yawned. 'Well, good luck to

the man and his urgent business. I'm off to bed!'

'We'll just have to draw and colour the posters for the walk ourselves,' Jenny shrugged, adding: 'I'll help you clear away, Mrs Grace.'

'No, Jen lass,' smiled her father. 'Don't you worry about that tonight. I'll give Ellen a hand. You go on and let Jess out for his last walk, then have an early night. You look sleepy.'

Jenny looked at her father. A soft, rather secretive, smile was hovering around the corners of his mouth. He looked very pleased with himself about something. 'OK, thanks,' she said. 'Goodnight. Thanks for supper!'

' 'Night, Jen, love,' Ellen Grace said softly.

Jess followed Jenny to the back door. He bounded through the porch, then stood wagging his tail, barking, as she pulled on her shoes. 'I'm coming as fast as I can!' Jenny chided him, laughing.

Jess ran over to where Nell and Jake, his parents, were dozing beside the barn. It was a warm spring evening, and Nell had made herself a little nest in a pile of discarded straw. Jake was curled up close to her. He thumped his tail in greeting when he saw the younger dog, who briefly touched noses with his mother, before running off into the field.

Jenny straightened and peered into the gathering gloom for Jess. She could just make out the woolly

shapes of the sheep, shuffling around at the fence along the top field, like small wintry clouds. She whistled, and Jess came streaking towards her.

Jess is more than a working dog, Jenny thought, *and much more than just a pet. He is, quite simply, the best dog in the whole world.*

Back inside, Jenny discovered that her father and Mrs Grace had gone into the sitting-room. The door was closed but she could hear the distant murmuring of their chatter. She shook out Jess's blanket and then laid it back in his basket.

Matt had come into the kitchen and was filling a

glass of water at the sink. 'What's going on, d'you think?' he said, with a quizzical smile on his face.

'What do you mean, going on?' Jenny frowned, puzzled.

'Dad and Mrs Grace seem . . . different together,' Matt said. 'You know, as though something has changed.'

'Well, Mrs Grace *does* look a bit dressed up this evening . . . and Dad is being especially nice to her. At dinner, I thought for a moment it might be her birthday!' Jenny grinned. 'Oh, Matt! You don't think . . .?'

'Romance is in the air?' Matt frowned. 'Maybe.'

'I guess it would make Dad happy,' Jenny said thoughtfully.

'I'm not so sure,' Matt replied. 'Dad has just begun to settle down and enjoy life again after Mum . . . I think he needs more time.'

'Maybe,' Jenny said. She looked at Jess as he got into his basket and curled up. 'Goodnight, Jess.'

'It's too soon,' Matt said, in a distant voice, as if he were talking to himself. He was still frowning.

'Oh, don't let's think about it now, Matt. We don't know for sure, do we? Besides, there's too much else going on. I'm not going to give it another thought! Let's just wait and see what happens.'

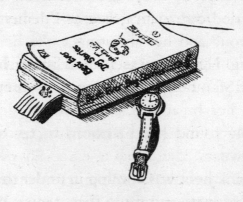

4

Jenny slept fitfully. She was deep in the clutches of a series of dreams.

In one, she was standing on the corner of a busy road in Greybridge, pleading with people passing by to sign up for her sponsored walk. In another, she was striding out along a stretch of smooth, tarred road. Carrie walked briskly beside her, a huge smile on her face. But the tar began to melt, and it grew stickier and stickier. The soles of their shoes began to melt into the tar and hold them fast, and Carrie stretched out her hand to Jenny. 'Help me, Jen,' she begged. 'I've got to make it. I've *got* to.'

Jenny cried out in her dream: 'I'm here Carrie. I'll help you!' and her shouting woke her. She sat up, gasping. Her hair was matted across her damp forehead. She blinked and took a deep breath to steady her breathing, then looked slowly and deliberately round her bedroom to try and calm herself down.

A soft pink light was coming in under the edge of her curtains. It was no more than a glow, but it was comforting. There was the photograph of her mother, smiling at her, and one of Jess, about ten weeks old. She pushed back her hair and went over to the window to pull back the curtains. A crescent of sun was starting to show above the horizon but the dawn chill gave her goosebumps. She scurried back into bed.

Monday mornings weren't the same without Carrie being in school, Jenny reflected. She didn't look forward to being there quite as much, although Fiona was a good friend to her. Pulling the blankets up to her throat, Jenny wished for the hundredth time that Carrie's operation had come and gone, and that her friend was better – that things were the way they used to be. The sadness she felt was like a weight, pressing down on her. It was as if it were trying to squeeze all the breath out of her.

She remembered that when Carrie had first been ill, Mrs Grace had given her some advice. 'Conjure up a picture of Carrie in happier days,' she had said, 'and hold on to the image in your mind.' Jenny tried this now, and into her head popped a vision of Carrie at the birthday party of a school friend the previous year. Her coppery hair flew around her face as she danced about, showing off a new dress her mum had bought her, and laughing.

A party! She would give Carrie a party! Jenny sat bolt upright in bed. It would be the perfect end to the day of the sponsored walk. Carrie would love it, Jenny felt sure. There would be streamers and balloons, delicious things to eat, music to dance to, and all of Carrie's friends and family there to wish her well for the operation.

Struck by the brilliance of this idea, Jenny snatched up her wristwatch, which was lying under her reading book on the bedside table. It read 5.45 am. Dad would be up and out in the fields, with Matt, by now. She would go and share the idea with them.

She dressed hurriedly, pulling on a pair of denims and a sweatshirt that was muddy from yesterday's walk with Jess. Then she tore out a page from her school jotter and scribbled a note to Mrs Grace: *I woke up early, so have gone out to see the lambs. Love, Jenny.*

The door to the housekeeper's bedroom was shut. Jenny slipped the note under it and took the stairs to the kitchen two at a time. Jess was curled into a tight little ball in his basket, his soft blue blanket tucked cosily round him. At the sound of Jenny's footsteps he lifted his head and peered sleepily up at her. His chin was propped on the edge of the basket and one eye was partially closed.

Jenny dropped to her haunches and kissed the top of his head. 'You coming, sleepyhead? I'm going out to the fields,' Jenny whispered.

Jess yawned and craned his neck up to the ceiling to stretch. Then, fully awake, he leaped out of his basket and ran to the kitchen door, wagging his tail. Jenny quietly opened the door to the porch and pulled on her wellington boots.

She found her father, with Matt, outside the shearing shed. Matt was shredding bales of straw with a pitchfork and Fraser Miles was putting the finishing touches to a new lamb incubator with a screwdriver. The sheepdogs, Nell and Jake, were lying side by side looking into the field that held over a hundred head of blackface sheep – watching for any movement that might be a signal for them to work. Jess took his cue from his parents, and lay down obediently nearby — his eyes never leaving Jenny.

'Hi!' said Jenny.

'Well, hello, lass!' Fraser Miles looked up in surprise. 'We don't usually see you up and about this early on a school morning.'

'Did you bring up a Thermos of coffee?' Matt demanded.

'No, I didn't,' Jenny replied. 'I've only come for a quick chat.' She peeped into the lambing box. 'No, orphans, Dad?'

'Not so far, Jenny, thankfully.' Fraser Miles grinned. As the lambing season progressed, there were usually a host of unlucky little new-borns whose mothers rejected them, refusing to feed or care for them. This was where the heated, wooden box Fraser Miles was working on came in. Jenny liked to think of it as a little hospital ward, in which the lambs could be kept safe and warm, and be fed by willing nurses, such as herself.

One year there had been so many needy new lambs that Jess had had to be employed as a surrogate mother. He had gone off around the fields with bottles of warm milk harnessed to his sides in an old waistcoat. The collie had done a brilliant job and had earned the admiration of all who heard the story.

'Well?' said Matt, wiping his forehead with a handkerchief, and grinning at his sister. 'Go on then, chat away.'

'Well, listen to this! I thought it would be a great idea to throw a big party for Carrie — after the sponsored walk, I mean.' Jenny sat down on a bale of hay and curled her legs under her. Matt and her father said nothing. 'What do you think?' Jenny prompted.

'I think it's a fine idea, Jen, lass,' Mr Miles said. 'I'm only thinking that Carrie might not feel well enough to dance a jig, you know . . .'

'Then she needn't,' Jenny explained. 'She can sit comfortably and be among all the people who care about her.'

'Sorry to have to be the practical one but what's it going to cost, this big party?' Matt wondered, making a face.

'We can all chip in,' Jenny explained. 'Us, and Mrs Grace and the Turners and the MacLays . . . I've got some pocket money saved.'

'You could have it in the village hall,' Matt said, warming to the idea.

'Yes,' Fraser Miles said thoughtfully, 'there's room enough there for a proper knees-up — a ceilidh, even.'

'It will be great fun,' Jenny said, getting up and jumping about excitedly. Jess came to her side immediately, rose up gracefully and put his front paws against her collarbone. She threw her arms round his neck. The more she thought about it, the clearer the picture of Carrie became, spinning around happily in her new dress at Laura Dern's party.

'Whoa!' said Mr Miles, holding up a calming hand. Jenny sat down, slightly out of breath. 'There's rather a lot to organise and sort out, Jenny. All this is going to take time and effort. There's the walk, now the party — and school in-between — not to mention all that's going on on the farm!'

'I can do it by myself,' Jenny promised. 'I won't need your help. I know you've got enough to do.' She jumped up again. 'But you're right, Dad. There is a lot to be done. I'd better get going.'

'See you later,' Matt called.

Jess sprang after his mistress as she raced away across the field, scattering the sheep in her path. After a minute, Jenny slowed to a jog. The pinky-orange sun was sliding higher into a clear dawn sky. It was going to be a lovely day.

There were posters to design and put up, invitations to write and food to plan, and all before Carrie had her operation. Afterwards, Jenny knew, her friend wouldn't be well enough to walk, or to dance.

This is the best way to show Carrie how much I care about her, Jenny thought. Her only regret was how little time she had had lately to help her father and brother with the farm. But it couldn't be helped. For the meantime, Carrie had to come first – and there wasn't a moment to lose.

A couple of hours later, Jenny discovered David waiting for her at the gates of their school.

'Hi,' Jenny called, hitching her schoolbag over her shoulder and striding towards him.

'Hi,' David replied, looking a bit awkward. He shuffled from foot to foot. 'You know, don't you, that I'll be coming to your house, later on, to stay for a bit? Is that all right with you?'

'That's fine!' Jenny smiled. 'We've got a room for you. How long is your dad going to be away?'

'I don't really know,' David mumbled. 'But I'm sure he won't be gone long. I'll go home after school and he'll bring me to your place later. OK?'

'That's fine,' Jenny said again, sensing that he wanted to be sure that she *really* didn't mind him sharing Windy Hill. 'It'll be great to have you – and Orla, of course. We'll have fun on the farm – and we can work together on planning the walk and . . . here's Fiona.' Jenny couldn't wait to tell Fiona about her idea for a party.

'Hello, you two.' Fiona hurried over, frowning. She looked tired. 'I haven't finished my homework! That science was so hard and—'

Jenny didn't give her a chance to finish. 'Listen, Fi! I've had a great idea!' She seized Fiona's arm. 'Why don't we give Carrie a surprise party at the end of the sponsored walk? We could do it in the village hall!'

'A party?' said Fiona. 'You mean, like a birthday party?'

'No, it's not her *birthday*, silly. Just a party – to wish her good luck and things with her operation.'

'That's a nice idea,' David said. 'I'd be on for that. But who will supply the music . . . food . . . drinks . . . and pay the bill?'

'We'll have to sort it all out,' Jenny said with determination. 'We've got time.'

'My mum will help,' Fiona suggested.

'We can tell Mrs Turner – in confidence,' Jenny said. 'She'll help.'

'There's the bell,' said David. 'We'd better go in. Let's talk about it more at break.'

As Jenny went into class, she had a little spring in her step. Automatically, she put out her hand to share her feelings with Jess, then realised that he wasn't there. *What a shame that dogs aren't allowed in school*, Jenny thought.

When Jenny got home at four o' clock, Ellen Grace was just leaving Windy Hill.

'It's my friend, Mrs Perry,' she told Jenny. 'She hasn't been well at all, poor thing. I said I'd do her shopping for her.'

Jess was prancing about, delighted that Jenny was home. He found her wellington boots and paraded about with one in his mouth. Jenny chuckled and rubbed his ears. 'Yes, I missed you, too!' she said.

'I won't be back late,' Ellen was edging her way round the dancing collie. 'I must hurry or I won't get to the chemist in time and . . . oh! Look, Jenny, here comes a visitor.'

Jenny looked out of the window. Sarah Taylor was getting out of her car. She waved and smiled at Jenny, then walked to the kitchen door. Mrs Grace got there first and greeted the young woman warmly.

'I'm afraid I'm just off, Sarah,' she explained. 'But Jenny's here. Come on in.'

'Hello, Sarah!' Jenny was pleased to see her, then added: 'See you later, Mrs Grace.'

'Bye, you two,' Ellen Grace said.

Sarah came into the kitchen and peeled off a light blue cardigan. As she smoothed Jess's black ears, her blonde hair swung round her shoulders. She perched on the end of the pine table and smiled at Jenny. 'I heard something about a sponsored walk for charity,' she said. 'Anything I can do?'

'Gosh! People are talking about it already! That's just what I hoped would happen,' Jenny said happily. 'I need as much help as I can get,' she admitted.

'Right,' said Sarah, slipping off the table. 'Then let's get started. Have you got a piece of paper and a pencil?'

Jenny usually gave Jess a long walk when she got home from school but now she settled down at the table to work on making a list of tasks. The collie seemed to sense something important was going on, so he lay down beside Jenny's chair and waited patiently.

'I feel much better now,' Jenny said gratefully, when she'd gone through all the details with Sarah. 'Not so worried about it all.'

'Carrie won't be having her operation for a few weeks yet,' Sarah said, 'so the Saturday we've picked for the walk is the best time. I think we'll be organised by then.'

'I want to give Carrie a party, after the walk,' Jenny said. 'It'll be a secret, so she'll get a real surprise. What do you think?'

'Good idea!' Sarah's face lit up. 'A knees-up might be just the thing to give her a boost before the operation.' She reached over to the little pad of paper and made a few more notes. 'I'll help you organise the party, too, if you like.'

'Thanks, Sarah.' Jenny's smile was radiant. She hadn't liked to ask Mrs Grace for help, and her dad was always so busy. She'd started to wonder how on earth she was going to make sure everything was done in time.

'Mrs Turner suggested that we donate the money we raise to the hospice where your sister stayed . . .'

'Oh, that's such a nice thought. Thank you. They could do with some help up there.' Sarah was beaming.

Jenny looked seriously at her. 'Is she . . . Carrie, going to be all right after the operation?' she asked.

'I can't say that for sure.' Sarah shook her head. 'But it's the best chance she has. The marrow in her own bones is breaking down – but as you know, my own marrow is the perfect match of cell tissue with hers, so it looks very positive.'

'Thank you,' Jenny said simply. 'Thanks for letting Carrie have some of it.'

'I'm glad to do it.' Sarah smiled. 'I'm what is known as MUD in medical terms, and I'm rather rare. MUD is Matched Unrelated Donor.'

Jenny smiled. 'Mud!' she said and wrinkled her nose. 'What's going to happen at the hospital?'

'It's really very simple,' Sarah explained. 'When all the drugs they are giving Carrie have done the job of destroying her damaged marrow, the marrow they get from me will be fed down a little tube and into her. Once the new cells are in Carrie's circulation, they find their own way to the places in the bone where the new marrow should establish itself. Then the doctors will have to check Carrie to make sure that new white blood cells are starting to be produced. If they are, then the transplant will have been successful.'

Jenny felt her head begin to ache. It seemed a lot to take in — and the thought of the operation *not* being successful made her feel sick.

'Well, I'd better be going now.' Sarah stood up. 'And don't worry about the walk or the party, Jenny — we'll make sure that Carrie has a great time.'

Jenny smiled. 'Thanks,' she said again. 'You've been brilliant.'

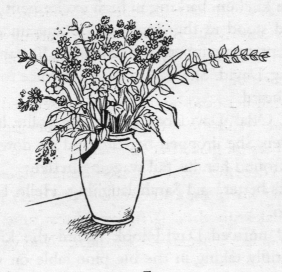

5

Just then, there was a soft knocking on the door. Jess went at once to investigate, his tail wagging and his head cocked to one side.

Jenny opened the door and gasped. David stood there, a small, black, bulging sports bag in his hand. 'Oh! David. I'd forgotten . . . the time! Come in.'

Jenny had been so intent on making plans, and talking to Sarah about Carrie, that David's arrival at Windy Hill had gone right out of her mind. There was a minute or two of confusion, as Orla rushed into the kitchen, barking in high excitement.

David stood in the doorway looking uncertain. Then Jenny remembered her manners. 'Let me take your bag, David.' She had to raise her voice to make herself heard.

'*Stop*, Orla!' David bellowed. The collie looked crestfallen. She dropped her ears and sat down. Jess walked round her, his tail wagging briskly.

'That's better,' said Sarah, laughing. 'Hello, David.'

'Hello.'

Jenny noticed David look round the kitchen rather stiffly, taking in the big pine table on which stood a vase stuffed full of wild flowers; the saucepans hung over the Aga range; and the brightly coloured cushions strewn along a wooden bench. It was a homely sort of room. Jenny guessed from the look on David's face that it was a very different kitchen from his own.

'I'm just on my way home,' Sarah told David. 'Jenny and I have been making plans for the walk. I'm sure she'll tell you all about it.' She picked up her cardigan.

'Thanks again, Sarah,' Jenny said.

'Bye.' Sarah smiled and slipped past David, who was still standing just inside the door. Orla was helping herself to a few biscuits left behind in Jess's breakfast bowl. When Jenny had closed the door, she wondered with a pang of guilt if Mrs Grace had had time to make up Ian's old room for David, and she remembered, too, that she had said she would help to prepare it. *Honestly, Jenny!* she chided herself. *This is not much of a welcome.*

'Did your dad bring you?' she asked cheerily.

'Yes, he dropped me at the gate. He was in a hurry.' David seemed hunched up inside his baggy jumper and his eyes darted round the room in a way that Jenny found unsettling. She thought it odd that Mr Fergusson hadn't had time to bring David in himself.

'Mrs Grace – she's our, sort of, housekeeper, and friend – will be back soon. Meantime, I'll take you upstairs to your room, if you like?' Jenny smiled. David seemed so ill-at-ease, she wasn't quite sure what to suggest.

'Yes, OK.' David stopped and took his bag from her. 'Is it all right if Orla sleeps in the kitchen? She's used to that.'

'Yes,' Jenny laughed, 'I'm sure Jess will feel very honoured.'

Jenny led David along the landing to a closed bedroom door. Inside, Mrs Grace had been true to her word, and Jenny found to her relief that she had made up the bed, removed the bits and pieces Ian had left behind in the wardrobe, and even put a few sprigs of lavender in a vase on the bookshelf.

'This is your room,' she told David. 'The bathroom's over there.'

'Thanks,' David said, managing a small smile. 'I'll just unpack my bag, then, OK?'

'Fine,' Jenny said. 'I'll be in the kitchen, doing my homework. I'll show you around the farm, when you're ready, and tell you all about our ideas for the walk, and the party.'

As she walked away down the landing, Jenny heard David firmly close the bedroom door. It made her feel uneasy. He *was* a hard person to get to know. And he seemed to be becoming more secretive as time went on!

Jess was sitting at the bottom of the stairs, looking up at Jenny as she came down. He thumped his tail, and looked across at Orla, who had curled up in his basket.

'Oh, Jess!' Jenny giggled, as she followed his gaze. 'She really has moved in, hasn't she? You're very kind to let her have your bed.' She stroked his silky head and he looked steadily up at her.

Jenny sat down on the bottom step and gave a big sigh. Jess put his nose lightly on her shoulder, edging closer for a cuddle, and her hair closed over his face like a curtain. She hugged the collie and felt a bit better. But there seemed a lot to deal with just now – Carrie, the walk, the party, her father's changing relationship with Mrs Grace, and now David, who was being rather sullen and difficult, too.

Jenny jumped when the telephone rang. She ran to answer it, hoping it might be Carrie. It was Fiona.

'Is he there? Has he come?' she demanded.

'Yes,' Jenny was guarded, thinking that David might appear on the stairs at any moment. She lowered her voice. 'He doesn't seem very happy at all,' she confided. 'His father left him at the bottom of the drive and went off. I mean, he doesn't even know where his son is going to sleep!'

'I tell you, there's something odd about it all,' Fiona sounded certain.

'Well, I'm being as nice as I can,' Jenny said. 'Maybe I can find out a little bit more about him and his dad.'

'Let me know what happens, won't you?' Fiona urged. 'Ring me later.'

'Fi,' Jenny chuckled, 'I'll see you at school tomorrow. I'll tell you then, OK?'

'Well, OK. But ring me if something dramatic happens.'

'Nothing *dramatic* is going to happen, silly,' Jenny whispered. 'Except that I'm going to get into a huge amount of trouble if I don't do my homework! And poor Jess hasn't even had his walk yet. See you tomorrow. Bye.'

'Bye.' Fiona hung up.

Jenny replaced the receiver and felt a little shiver go through her. What if Fiona was right? What if David and his father *were* criminals, on the run from the police? The more Jenny thought about this possibility, the more it seemed likely. There had been very few answers to the questions Jenny had asked about David's life before he moved to Cliffbay; Mr Fergusson seemed a really mysterious character, who was out of work one minute and rushing off on urgent business the next – and he called David *Douglas*! It just didn't add up.

Jenny found herself looking over her shoulder nervously, as she heard the creak of the wooden stairs. David came slowly into the kitchen, a blank expression on his face. For a second, Jenny was tongue-tied. She wished Mrs Grace had been there to make things easier. *This is ridiculous!* Jenny told herself. *It's just my imagination running wild.*

'Do you want to have a look around the farm?' she asked brightly.

David nodded. And then Jess did something that made Jenny feel a lot happier. He went over to David and, very gently, put his nose in the palm of the boy's hand. David, looking surprised, gave Jess a loving stroke, murmuring: 'Hello, Jess. Good boy!'

'Well,' said Jenny, 'that's Jess's way of saying welcome!' Instantly she remembered the way the collie had sensed the evil intent in Marion, a former friend of her father's, who had come to stay at Windy Hill last year. Jess had been wary of the woman from the start – and he had been right. She had ended up trying to poison him for her own selfish gain. Surely Jess's fine instinct would sense if David, in some way, was going to mean trouble for the Mileses?

'Come on, then.' Jenny smiled in relief. 'Let's get going. Jess needs his walk. I'll show you the lambs first, shall I?'

Orla and Jess bounded along as Jenny led the way round the farm. As they walked, Jenny chattered on about the lambing, the dipping and the shearing, pointing out bits of equipment and all the technical terms that she thought might interest David. She told him about Darktarn Keep, and the horse, Mercury. He seemed to relax as he listened, and the strained look on his face finally melted into a smile.

'It's nice here,' he said, looking across the sloping hills to the sea. 'I'd like to live on a farm.'

'You do – for now!' Jenny chuckled. 'You can explore any part of it – and help my dad too, if you want.'

'Thanks,' David said. He rubbed his fingers through his hair. 'Where's your mother?' he asked suddenly.

Jenny was startled. She hadn't realised David didn't know the Mileses' history. 'Um . . . she died . . . in a riding accident, two years ago.' She spoke quietly.

'Mine too,' David mumbled.

'Really?' Jenny was stunned. She had imagined that the absent Mrs Fergusson had married another man, but she had never liked to ask. 'Horse riding . . .?'

'No – in a car.' David looked away, and the shadow Jenny had seen so often crept across his face, darkening his eyes.

'It's horrible, isn't it, losing a mum?' she said simply.

'Yes.' He sighed. 'I've got Orla, though. I got her as a puppy after my mother died.'

'What a coincidence! I got Jess quite soon after my mum died, too,' Jenny smiled.

He looks so lonely, she thought. 'Does your father go away often – on business?' Jenny asked tentatively. She opened the door of the lower barn, where the newer lambs were kept until they were strong enough to go out to the field.

David went inside ahead of her. 'Not too often,' he

THE GIFT

said. 'Half the time I don't know when he's going or why he has to go – or even how long he'll be away!'

'How come?' Jenny frowned.

'Look,' David said, suddenly turning on her. 'I don't want to talk about my father, or what he does, or why. OK? Let's just leave it.' He pushed past Jenny and went over to an enclosure, where he dropped onto his knees in the straw, peering in at the lambs, so Jenny couldn't see his face.

She was so surprised she didn't know what to do. She just stood there, gaping after him. But Jess's cold nose roused her. He was nudging at her, looking up, as if he was trying to tell her something. Then, the collie went over to David, sat down in the straw beside him and held up a paw. David half turned, and took Jess's front foot, with its little white sock, gently in his hand.

There! thought Jenny. *Jess is showing me that I should try to understand David. Jess trusts him and so should I.*

She walked to where David was kneeling. 'I'm really sorry,' she said. 'I didn't mean to pry. I won't ask any more questions, OK?'

David smiled sheepishly. 'I'm sorry I got cross. Are these new-born lambs?' he said, changing the subject.

Jenny nodded. 'Do you want to hold one?'

★ ★ ★

When the lights came on in the kitchen at the farmhouse, Jenny and David made their way home from the top field. They found Mrs Grace out of breath, rushing round the kitchen trying to hurry a meal together.

'Oh, David! Hello!' she said. 'I'm sorry I was so long! I wanted to be here when you arrived.' She threw some pasta into a pan of simmering water.

'It doesn't matter, Mrs Grace,' Jenny smiled. 'David's settled in, and I've shown him around. How's Mrs Perry?'

'Not well at all. I ended up by taking her to her doctor. Is your room all right, David?' she asked.

'Fine, thank you,' David replied.

'I'm sorry I didn't see your father, but . . .' She broke off, and her face broke into a beaming smile, as Fraser Miles came striding in through the kitchen door, bringing with him the strong smell of sheep. Jess hurried over to greet him.

'Ah! Hello, David. Welcome to Windy Hill.' Mr Miles spoke warmly, putting out a hand to pat the Border collie.

'Thanks Mr Miles.' David looked a little overwhelmed. He looked from Jenny, to Mrs Grace, to Mr Miles.

Jenny decided it would help if she gave him

something to do. 'Will you help me to set the table for supper?' she asked, going over to a large oak dresser. David followed and Jenny handed him the cutlery as she pulled it out of the drawer. 'There's five of us, so . . .'

'Um, there's just the *three* of you tonight.' Fraser Miles corrected, clearing his throat. Jenny looked at her father, confused.

'How come?' she asked.

'I've decided to take Ellen out . . . to a restaurant,' he finished quietly.

'Then . . . something special has happened! It must have! What are we . . . you . . . celebrating?' Jenny cried, turning to Mrs Grace.

Ellen Grace chuckled as she stirred a cheese sauce. 'Nothing, Jenny. Your father and I just thought it would make a pleasant change, that's all.'

David was standing still, holding the knives and forks in his hand. Quickly, Jenny swallowed her surprise. 'Well, good. That's . . . lovely. We'll be fine, here,' she mumbled.

Jenny suddenly noticed now that Mrs Grace was wearing a new dress, one she hadn't seen before.

'Matt will be in soon,' her father said. 'You can all eat together and watch a bit of telly. I'm going upstairs to change.'

'Fine, Dad,' Jenny said. She took the cutlery from David, feeling a slight flush creep into her cheeks. This was a first – her dad taking Mrs Grace out on a date! And on the very night that David Fergusson had arrived to stay! Things seemed to be changing at Windy Hill – and Jenny wasn't certain that she was completely happy about it.

Later, when she, Matt and David, had demolished the last of Mrs Grace's cheesy pasta, she left David watching television in the sitting-room with Jess and Orla and went upstairs to find her brother. A thin line of light was showing from under his bedroom door. Jenny went straight in.

'Do come in,' Matt said mockingly. 'And thanks for knocking.'

'Sorry,' Jenny said, and sat down on the end of the bed, frowning.

'What's up?' Matt asked, stacking a pile of his college books into a bag.

'Dad's never been out for *dinner* with Mrs Grace before,' Jenny stated.

'I think I was right,' he said, nodding his head. 'Romance is definitely on the cards for those two.'

'I've been thinking about it,' Jenny said. 'I don't feel . . . right . . . about having another . . . mother

. . . living here at Windy Hill. I know Mum isn't actually here, Matt, but, even so, she might not like it if someone takes her place in the family.'

'I know what you mean,' Matt said kindly. 'I wasn't sure how I felt about it at first, but Mrs Grace wouldn't be a mum, would she? She'd be a stepmother.'

'What's the difference?' Jenny asked. 'It still seems as if our mum is being replaced, somehow.'

'Think of it this way,' Matt suggested. 'Mum wouldn't want Dad to be lonely, and alone, for the rest of his life, would she?'

'He's not alone!' Jenny said tearfully. Her face was hot. 'He's got me – and you!'

'And Mrs Grace,' Matt finished. He slipped an arm round his sister's shoulders. 'She's been great, to us – all of us. But I know how you feel. It doesn't seem very long ago that Mum was still here, and now . . .'

But Jenny couldn't listen to another word. Her world seemed to be tilting. Everything she had been sure of was changing. Suddenly it seemed too much. She covered her face with her hands and began to cry.

'We're still a family,' Matt soothed. 'There'll always be Dad, and me and you . . . and Mum, somewhere, watching over us . . .'

'And Jess,' Jenny added, through her tears.

'And Jess,' Matt agreed. 'Mrs Grace is a . . . bonus! She's an added extra! The cherry on top of the cake.'

In spite of herself, Jenny giggled. 'You're right,' she said. 'Mrs Grace is every bit as good as a mum, without actually being Mum.'

'Let's give her a chance, Jen,' Matt urged. 'Anyway, you've got more important things to worry about at the moment than something that might never happen.'

'Yes,' Jenny wiped her eyes on her sleeve. 'Carrie.'

'Carrie,' Matt repeated. 'There's a lot to do, remember?'

'Thanks Matt. I'll get some sleep now, and tomorrow I'll really get organised!'

6

It had been the busiest two weeks Jenny could remember. When she woke up on the morning of the sponsored walk, she went over all the details of the day ahead, one last time.

Sponsorship forms had been given out in handfuls, and Jenny was certain there would be a good turnout for the walk. The village hall had been decked out in metres of bright bunting and balloons. Food, prepared by friends and members of Carrie's family, had been arriving secretly over the last couple of days and filled the big chest freezer in the garage at Windy Hill. A traditional band had been booked for the party, too.

Mrs Grace, with Mrs Turner, Mrs MacLay and Sarah, had worked tirelessly, making sure the hired glasses were polished and that the beautiful cake for Carrie was iced to perfection. They had gone about it all so carefully that, in spite of all the unavoidable hustle and bustle, Carrie knew nothing about the evening celebration to come.

It had been David's job to cycle around Graston, sticking up posters wherever he could. 'Nearly everyone in the village knows my face now,' he had told Jenny, arriving back at Windy Hill one evening after a poster-sticking session. 'It's been a great way to make friends.'

Jenny was satisfied that they had all done their best to make it a successful occasion. Even Jess had played his part. Her constant companion as always, the collie had kept Jenny's spirits up when tiredness overwhelmed her. Her only aching worry was Carrie herself, who hadn't been at all well during the last week. The amount of drugs she had been receiving for her illness had been increased, to prepare her body for her transplant, and it had left her feeling weaker and sicker than before.

'Twenty tablets a day,' Carrie had made a ghastly face as she reported this to Jenny. 'You can have it in a liquid medicine, but it tastes too disgusting to drink.'

'Can't you crush the tablets up into something sickly sweet to drown out the taste?' Jenny had asked.

'I've tried it.' Carrie had smiled weakly.

Jenny hoped that Carrie would be well enough to see the walkers set off from Graston post office, even if she wasn't able to walk any distance herself. Jenny wanted her to be there, at least, at the start. The sight of all those people, striding out with Carrie's cause as their inspiration, would boost her spirits, Jenny felt sure. Jess would be sporting a bunch of brightly coloured ribbons – bought for him by Vicky, Matt's girlfriend. All that remained to be done was to give Jess's coat a thorough brushing, so that it would gleam in the sun as he trotted along.

Jenny put on her dressing-gown and went down into the kitchen to groom the collie. To her surprise, Jess wasn't there. His basket was empty. The open kitchen door creaked as it moved in a gentle, early morning breeze. She went to the door and looked out. It was unlike Jess to go off early with her father or Matt. There was no sign of Mrs Grace, either.

The house felt strangely empty without her usual morning greeting.

'Jess!' Jenny called. 'Here, boy! Mrs Grace?'

Ellen Grace's voice came back immediately. 'Over here, Jenny. We're behind the barn.'

Puzzled, Jenny began to hurry across the dewy grass in her bare feet. 'What's happened?' she called out.

'Don't worry . . .' said Mrs Grace, then: 'Wait, Jess, stay still . . . good boy!'

Jenny's heart leaped up into her throat. Was something wrong with Jess? She rushed round the corner of the barn. Mrs Grace was crouching over Jess, who was lying on his side. He looked forlornly up at Jenny as she gasped, 'Oh! What's the matter with him?'

'Nothing at all,' Ellen Grace said reassuringly. 'He wanted to be let out very early this morning and I was making some tea when I heard him give a mighty yelp. He's got a nasty splinter of wood in his paw, poor thing.'

'Oh, Jess!' Jenny knelt down and peered at the collie's paw. The shard of wood had pierced the skin of the pad deeply. Mrs Grace held up Jess's foot, wielding a pair of eyebrow tweezers as deftly as a dentist. She gripped, twisted and pulled – and finally

the splinter came out. Jess yelped again as a blob of
bright red blood welled up.

'There!' said the housekeeper triumphantly,
stroking Jess. 'Poor wee boy!' She took a small lacy
handkerchief from her pocket and dabbed tenderly
at the collie's bleeding foot, then dropped a kiss on
the top of his head.

'Will he be able to walk?' Jenny asked, stroking
him.

'He'll be fine,' Mrs Grace said, standing back to let
Jess up. The collie got to his feet and took a few
paces, holding up his front left paw as he did so. 'But
I'll go in and find some antiseptic ointment to put

on the wound to stop it getting infected.'

As Mrs Grace turned to go, Jenny noticed that the knees of her trousers were soiled with mud, and that there was blood on her sleeve. Jess was looking up at the housekeeper with warm, gold-brown eyes, his tail swaying slowly. Carefully, he tried out the injured foot by putting it onto the ground and taking a step. Then he wagged his tail harder.

He's going to be all right to do the walk! Jenny thought happily. On a sudden impulse, she reached up and gave Ellen Grace a hug.

The squeeze was affectionately returned. 'What's that for?' Mrs Grace chuckled, looking into Jenny's face.

'I just want to say . . . that I'm *really* glad you live with us and that . . . I hope you'll stay,' Jenny blurted.

Ellen Grace patted the top of Jenny's fair head. 'I might,' she smiled. 'You know, I just might.'

Clusters of people were standing about outside the post office when Jenny arrived with her dad, Mrs Grace, David, Matt and the two dogs. She recognised several of the teachers from school, and the faces of a few of the others were familiar too.

'There's Mrs Linden from the doctor's rooms,' said Mrs Grace, 'and Mr Cole from the bakery.'

'Gosh,' said Jenny, 'Look! Even our headmaster is here.'

As the crowd of walkers began to swell, Jenny saw that a few members of the local police were milling about, smiling and nodding, and keeping an eye out for the safety of younger children. They were putting up a cordon of red tape to keep the cars away. Fiona arrived, with her entire family, and lots of Jenny's classmates. Jess kept close to Jenny's side, though Orla was straining on her lead to reach him. Paul MacLay carried Toby under one arm, and the little Border terrier was shivering all over with excitement.

Jenny looked about, eager to see Carrie. There was no sign of Mr or Mrs Turner, and Jenny's hopes were beginning to sink.

'She'll make it – you'll see,' Matt said, giving Jenny's arm a little squeeze.

'Nearly time to start. Oh, but where's Carrie?!' Fiona was standing on tiptoe, trying to see over the heads of the crowd.

Jenny shrugged. 'Hasn't come – but she might. She only said she would see how she felt, Fi, remember?'

'Shh!' David hissed. 'Look, Mr Hearn is going to say something!'

Mr Hearn, the headmaster of Greybridge, had climbed up onto a small wooden box so he could be seen. 'Ladies and gentlemen, boys and girls,' he boomed. 'Thank you all for coming today to attempt this walk, for an excellent cause. The weather is fine, the planned route is a beautiful one, so please enjoy yourselves and take care. You may begin . . . NOW!'

People immediately started to surge forward, jostling Jenny. She stood still, craning her neck, staring about and willing Carrie to be there, but there was no sign of any of the Turners. She was bitterly disappointed.

'Come on!' David urged her. 'You'll get left behind.' Jenny hurried to catch him up, and began to walk in line with her father, Mrs Grace and Matt. Jess, his beautiful ribbons dancing in the breeze, pranced along eagerly and Jenny was relieved to see that his injured foot was giving him no trouble.

'I'm sorry you're disappointed,' Mrs Grace said, slipping her arm through Jenny's. 'You know Carrie would have been here if she possibly could have.'

'It would have made her so happy to see all these people, from all over Graston and Cliffbay, and all the teachers, too, and . . .' she trailed off.

'I know,' Mrs Grace said soothingly. 'But Carrie will hear about it from you, and Fiona and David. You can describe this wonderful turn-out to her. It will be as good as if she herself had been here.'

Jenny wasn't convinced. But she pushed aside her misery and looked about her. Already the walkers were beginning to peel off the outer layers of their clothing. Jumpers were being stuffed into backpacks and tied round waists. There was a cool freshness to the morning, but the spring sun was starting to climb, and the strenuous pace of the walking was making people warm.

'Jenny!' Sarah Taylor was pushing her way through the throng of people striding along.

'Hello, Sarah!' Jenny said. 'I wondered where you were.'

'A bit late, I'm afraid,' Sarah said apologetically. 'There are so many people here! Isn't it great?'

'Yes,' Jenny admitted. 'But no Carrie.'

Sarah's face clouded over. 'What a shame,' she said. 'I had really hoped . . .'

'Me too,' Jenny said grimly.

They walked on, following the road as it began to wind around the headland and dip away down towards Cliffbay. David kept pace with Jenny, and Orla trotted along, side by side, with Jess. Jenny smiled at him, thinking how well they had got along at Windy Hill together after the sharp words that had been spoken the first day.

'Ouch!' David said. 'I think I've got a stone in my

trainer.' He stepped to the side to allow the stream of walkers to go past him and Jenny hung back, waiting while he untied his shoelace. Jess licked the side of his face as he crouched there, nearly causing him to topple over.

'Ugh! Silly boy!' David laughed.

I totally trust David now, Jenny thought, watching the collie's display of affection. *There's nothing strange about him at all – except his father!* 'Jess really likes you,' she said, pleased, as she gazed around her at the many determined faces. Then she felt her heart suddenly squeeze up tight in her chest. 'David! Look!' she cried.

David stood up and looked over to where Jenny was pointing. The crowd behind them had parted, to make way for someone who was forging a speedy path through its midst. Jess barked joyfully, his tail wagging hard.

'It can't be . . .' Jenny said, clutching onto David's sleeve. 'But . . . it is! It's Carrie!' she shouted at the top of her voice. 'Dad, Matt, Sarah, Fiona . . . everyone! Carrie's here! On her roller-skates!'

The others turned round and stopped in their tracks as the painfully thin figure with the little woollen beret sped towards them, a gleeful grin on her face. A cheer went up from the crowd which gradually parted to allow Carrie through.

Jenny saw the look of determination on her friend's face. Mr Turner, on one side of his daughter, and Mrs Turner, on the other, were supporting her under each arm, and jogging along to keep pace with the rolling wheels.

'Jenny!' Carrie yelled. 'I'm here. I made it!'

Jess dashed forward, prancing and leaping in welcome. Fraser Miles began to clap Carrie, and the applause was taken up slowly by the crowd. Within seconds, it erupted down the length and breadth of the group of walkers and became a roar of approval.

Carrie flushed with embarrassment, but looked delighted. Running forward to hug her, Jenny remembered not to squeeze her too tight. 'You *did* make it! I'm so glad,' she shouted above the sound of clapping and cheering. 'And what a good idea!' She pointed at the roller-skates.

'Are you going all the way, young lady?' Fraser Miles asked in a teasing tone. Jenny noticed that Mrs Turner was out of breath and looked pale with tiredness. 'If so, I'd be delighted to escort you.' He bowed playfully.

Carrie turned to her mum, who smiled at Mr Miles. 'That OK, Mum?'

'I suppose I could do with stopping for a rest,' she

said. 'It was quite a dash from the post office to catch you up. So, Carrie, if you're sure?'

'I'm sure,' said Carrie, her eyes shining. She held out her hand to Fraser Miles.

'I'll go on the other side, if you like, Mr Turner?' Matt stepped up, grinning.

'Suits me. Thanks, Matt,' Mr Turner puffed. 'I warn you, it's hard work.'

Carrie, supported by Mr Miles and Matt, looked around, smiling. 'Right,' she said. 'What are we waiting for? Let's go, shall we?'

Jenny began to jog along beside her friend. She glanced down at Jess's glossy head, and as the collie looked up at her, she could have sworn he was smiling.

7

'Here they come!' Matt shouted, his nose to the window of the village hall. Saturday evening had arrived at last, and Jenny, her calf muscles stiff from her ten kilometre walk, sprang to Matt's side and peered out.

First, she looked for Jess. His sleek shape was silhouetted against the darkening sky, his nose raised to the dusk air, as he sat in the back of the farm pick-up. He had enjoyed the sponsored walk, but Jenny guessed he was quite happy to be resting now, out there in the cool evening.

Jenny scanned the carpark for the Turners. 'Carrie's in the car! She's made it – again!' she said happily. She had been worried that Carrie would have felt exhausted after her marathon roller-skate, and would have stayed at home to rest.

Mrs Turner's orange mini, with the sunflower painted on the roof, pulled onto the gravel outside. The buzz of chattering and laughing dried up, and people began to duck down to hide behind chairs and tables. Members of the band had tucked themselves away behind a red velvet curtain, drawn across a small wooden stage, and Jenny saw one of them peep out and give the thumbs-up sign to a friend.

'Right,' said Matt, who was still at the window, monitoring what was going on outside. 'Carrie is getting out of the car . . . frowning hard . . . probably asking her parents why they've brought her here! Mr Turner's hand is on the door, and here she comes . . . now!'

Carrie's puzzled face appeared in the doorway, flanked by her parents. There was a terrific cheer from the crowd – which made her jump – as people began to appear from all corners of the big room. 'Surprise!'

Carrie's mouth fell open and her hand flew to cover it, as friends hurried forward to hug her and draw her into the room. She stood looking around, her big green eyes blinking slowly. A sunny smile appeared on her face, as she took in all the familiar faces, the table groaning with a spread of food, the streamers, balloons and the band. As the musicians began to play, she caught Jenny's eye. 'Did you do this?' she asked wonderingly, as Jenny came over.

'Me, and Sarah and David and Fiona and, oh, *loads* of us. We thought you could do with a bit of fun.' Jenny said. She was filled with relief and excitement. She tucked her arm through Carrie's. 'I'm so glad you're here!' she grinned.

'But I'm still wearing my sweaty old trainers and leggings!' Carrie groaned, patting her beret into place. 'And look at you!'

Jenny looked down at her own party dress and shrugged. 'If we'd asked you to change your clothes after the walk, it would have given away the secret,' she said. 'Anyway, how are you feeling after having roller-skated ten kilometres today?'

'Not too bad, though my ankles are a bit sore from the boots,' Carrie said. 'And I think I need to sit down.'

The moment she found a chair, friends crowded

round to congratulate Carrie for having completed the sponsored walk. Mr Miles appeared with a drink, and Fiona brought over a plate of small triangular sandwiches.

'But you *must* be hungry after that walk!' she said, when Carrie refused the offer of food.

'Nope,' Carrie said, watching as people began to dance. 'I just want to sit and look. I can't believe my eyes! How come I didn't find out about this?'

Jenny giggled. 'Clever planning,' she said. She was pleased with the result of her hard work. Everyone had come, even a few of the teachers from school – Mrs Teale and Mr Wallis, and Mr Hearn, the headmaster, with his wife. The dull little hall looked bright and welcoming – and even the music wasn't too loud, as Mrs Grace had feared it would be.

She looked over to see Matt inspecting a pile of sponsorship forms. Mrs Grace was helping him by tapping numbers into a pocket calculator, while Fraser Miles and Mr Turner were pouring drinks. Sarah was deep in conversation with a grey-haired woman Jenny knew to be Mrs Thom, who ran the hospice where Sarah's sister Katie had stayed.

'Look,' she pointed her out to Carrie. 'We're going to give the money raised to the lady talking with Sarah, over there.'

'Do we know how much was raised yet?' Mrs Turner asked, coming over with a bowl of crisps.

'No,' said Jenny, 'but Matt and Mrs Grace are adding it up now. I'll bet it's a lot. The path to Cliffbay was jam-packed with people.'

'Where's Jess?' Carrie asked suddenly, looking up at Jenny.

'Outside, in the back of the pick-up truck,' Jenny said. 'Dad didn't think it was a good idea to have him in the hall right at the start of the party. But he's waited long enough, now. I'll go and get him.'

Jenny crossed the hall and opened the door to the carpark. The music and the laughter followed her out into the chilly, deepening blue of dusk. Jess, still sporting his multicoloured ribbons, was sitting up in the back of the open pick-up, alert for any sign of Jenny. He stood up, wagging his tail, when he saw her. But there was someone sitting beside him in the van.

'David?' Jenny was alarmed. David's dark head was bent, his knees drawn up. 'Is everything OK?'

'I thought he might be lonely,' David said. 'We've been watching the stars come out, haven't we, Jess?' He ran the palm of his hand down the collie's back.

'Well, that's . . . nice of you!' Jenny was touched. 'I've come to take Jess inside now. Everyone's arrived.

You know, you really should have brought Orla.'

'No,' David shook his head. 'Orla isn't like Jess. She wouldn't be able to behave herself at a party the way he can. Anyway, she's tired after that walk. You know,' he added dreamily, 'I think Orla really likes staying at Windy Hill, with Jess, and everything.'

'We like having her too – and *you*, of course,' Jenny said warmly.

It was true, Jenny reflected. It had been much more fun having David around than she thought it would. He had grown more relaxed as the time went on, and had shown himself to be a willing helper, both on the farm and round the house – impressing Mrs Grace no end last Sunday morning by making a pile of pancakes for breakfast!

'Come on,' Jenny said, 'Let's go back in, now, or Carrie will be wondering what's happened to us. And, thanks for looking out for Jess,' she added.

'That's all right,' David said, jumping down from the van. He brushed the bits of straw and the dust from the back of his trousers with his hands. Jess waited, cocking his head at Jenny.

'Yes, come on, Jess,' she instructed and he leaped down, shook himself all over, then began to trot happily in the direction of the hall.

David has become my friend, Jenny realised, as she

followed. *I don't know very much about him — except that, like me, he loves his dog and, like me, he misses his mother, but I know that I've made a special friend.*

Carrie was still in the chair where Jenny had left her. Her cheeks were flushed and her eyes bright and happy. She was clapping in time to the music as the dancers whirled around her.

Walking in front of Jenny, Jess threaded his way through the throng to Carrie's side and put his nose in her lap, looking up at her and swishing his long, plumy tail. Smoothing his head, she slipped him a cheesy biscuit as a treat. The collie licked the last

crumbs from his muzzle, then turned and walked away from Carrie, looking back at her over his shoulder. He stopped, and barked sharply, once.

'Jess!' Jenny hissed. But the collie seemed determined. He came back to Carrie, looked up at her face, then turned and walked away a second time, stopping to look back at her and bark once more.

'He wants you to go with him,' Jenny explained. 'Do you feel well enough to follow?'

As Carrie got slowly out of the chair, Jess gently took hold of the sleeve of her sweatshirt with his teeth and, walking backwards, tugged her to the edge of the circle of dancers. Carrie began to giggle helplessly. She half turned to look back at Jenny, and shrugged, as if to say: 'What's he *doing*?' But having reached the dance floor, Jess dropped Carrie's sleeve and trotted back to Jenny.

Carrie's waist was immediately encircled by Mrs MacLay on one side, and Sarah on the other. As she was swept up into the ring of dancers and whirled away, Jenny heard her laugh pealing through the room.

'You're *so* special!' Jenny told Jess, laughing and hugging the collie.

'That dog!' Fraser Miles shook his head wonderingly. Then he asked: 'Is Carrie having a good time?' He bent down to talk in Jenny's ear as she sat looking at Carrie.

'Yes, I think she is, Dad,' Jenny said happily.

'And you, Jenny? Are you enjoying the party?' he asked, putting a hand on her shoulder.

'I am.' Jenny smiled.

'Do you want to dance with your old dad?' Mr Miles asked.

'No thanks,' Jenny said 'But I know someone who might. Mrs Grace!'

'Ah, well, now, I think she's a bit busy for . . .' he began, looking disconcerted.

Jenny interrupted. 'No, she isn't, Dad. She'd *love* to dance. Go on, ask her, please! Or I'll get Jess to take you to her,' she threatened, teasingly.

Mr Miles looked suddenly determined. 'All right then, I will!' He handed his glass to his daughter, and surged away through the crowd to Ellen Grace's side. Jenny saw her hurriedly take the last bite of a sandwich, as Fraser Miles led her to the dance floor.

'Your dad is *dancing* with Mrs Grace!' Fiona pointed out.

Jenny nodded, smiling. 'And about time, too,' she said.

Ellen Grace was gazing up at Fraser as she danced,

her eyes wide, a soft, rather secretive, smile on her face. She looked different Jenny thought, though she wasn't sure why. Again, she had the feeling that something had changed – for ever.

A small shiver went through Jenny. Jess edged a little closer to her side and her fingers found the soft tufts of fur on his chest.

She could not remember seeing her father as happy for ages – since her mum was alive, in fact. She sat back on her wooden chair with a sigh of pleasure.

Carrie was still dancing when Mr Turner brought the hall to sudden stillness by rapping on the table. He asked for the attention of the guests, then raised his voice to be heard. 'Carrie's mother and I want to thank you all for making this a day – and a night – to remember. You all deserve our gratitude, but we would like to say a special thank you to Sarah Taylor, whose courage has given our Carrie real hope for a healthy, and happier, future.'

Mr Turner's voice quavered as he lifted a huge, cellophane-wrapped bouquet of flowers and handed it to Sarah. Colour flamed into her face as she hurried forward to cries of: 'Well done Sarah!' and 'Good luck for the operation!' and 'We'll be thinking of you both.' Then, Sarah beckoned to Mrs

Thom, who came forward to accept the money that had been collected from the walk.

'Oh!' said Mrs Thom, as she looked at the amount on the cheque. 'This is amazing – much more than I expected! Thank you all, so very much.'

When the music started up again, Carrie was persuaded by her father to try a lively Scottish reel and Jenny danced with Matt, and then her father. She kept an eye out for Jess, who wandered slowly among the guests, enjoying the strokes and attention he got, and the tasty nibbles that were slipped his way.

Then, suddenly, it had gone midnight, and Jenny was struggling to keep her eyelids open.

Carrie's face was pale, the shadows like bruises under her eyes. Mrs Turner gave Jenny a hug as they left and Carrie said: 'I'll do the same for you, one day, Jen!' and grinned at her sleepily.

Jenny couldn't wait to go home to bed. It had been a wonderful day, one that she would never forget, but the effort of the last two weeks had finally caught up with her. She was exhausted!

Back at Windy Hill, Ellen Grace began to cover the leftover food and wash up the hired glasses. 'I'd rather do it now than have to face it in the morning,' she said gently, when Fraser Miles suggested that it was far too late at night for kitchen chores. 'You go on up to your beds – all of you.'

'If you're sure, Ellen.' Jenny's dad climbed the stairs gratefully.

'I can't stand on my legs another minute,' David confessed, yawning.

'Goodnight!' Ellen chuckled. 'Sleep tight.'

Jenny untied Jess's ribbons and he curled up in his basket, yawning. Then she followed Matt upstairs.

'Jenny! Matt!' Mr Miles called from his bedroom. 'Come in here for a moment, will you?'

Matt looked at Jenny and raised his eyebrows. The bedroom door was ajar, and Mr Miles was pacing under the window.

'What's up, Dad?' Matt asked, sitting on the edge of the bed.

Jenny sat beside him, rubbing her eyes. 'I'm so sleepy, Dad . . . I don't think . . .'

'This won't take a minute,' Jenny's father spoke hurriedly. He looked flustered and uncomfortable. 'I just wanted to know how . . . you would feel . . . if I asked Ellen to marry me?'

Jenny's heavy eyelids flew wide open and she gasped. An unexpected feeling of joy surged through her and she leaped off the bed and ran to hug her father. 'Yes!' she said. 'Oh, yes! It feels . . . *right*. It *is* right. Yes!'

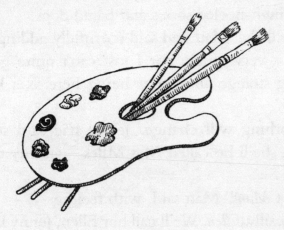

8

Jenny slept deeply and woke up late, to the smell of bacon frying. Her first thought was about her father's announcement the night before. Part of her felt sad – wishing things didn't have to happen so fast. But then she thought about Ellen Grace – her warm blue eyes, and the way she loved Jess and Windy Hill – and realised how lucky a family they were to have found her.

'After all,' she had reasoned, as she sat on Matt's bed late the previous night, 'Dad might have chosen someone completely unsuitable – someone who wore high-heeled shoes and hated dogs.'

'Unlikely!' Matt had said scornfully, adding: 'I like her . . . very much, but I just can't quite get over feeling strange about her being here as a kind of *mother*.'

'Nothing will change,' Jenny had said sensibly. 'Only, she'll be called Mrs Miles – and *we* can call her . . .'

'Not *Mum*!' Matt said, with feeling.

'No, silly. *Ellen*. We'll call her Ellen,' Jenny had said decisively, and smiled.

Now, she stretched contentedly as she lay in her bed. Her legs ached from yesterday's strenuous walk but her spirits were high. She would suggest to David that they walk Jess and Orla along the path to Cliffbay. She wished it were possible for Carrie to come along, but after the celebration the day before, Jenny doubted that Carrie would have any remaining energy for a long walk.

When Jenny went down to the kitchen, her fair head tousled from sleep and her feet bare, Mrs Grace was humming to herself. Jenny went straight over and put her arms round Ellen's waist. 'Dad told us – last night. I'm really pleased,' she said simply, squeezing tight. 'You *are* going to say yes, aren't you?'

'I already have!' Mrs Grace laughed. 'Of course!'

'This means you're going to stay at Windy Hill for ever, doesn't it?' Jenny urged.

'I hope so, Jenny,' Mrs Grace smiled. 'And I'm very pleased that you're pleased.'

'Can Matt and I call you Ellen now?' Jenny asked, stooping to say good morning to Jess, who had brought her a slipper. Orla was having a long drink from the big stone bowl under kitchen counter. 'It would be odd to say Mrs Miles.'

'Yes, it does sound odd. Ellen will be fine,' she replied.

'Are you going to have a proper wedding – a huge reception and all that?' Jenny wanted to know.

'Well, not *too* big,' Ellen smiled. 'For one thing, big weddings cost an awful lot of money. And my family are all too far away to come to Scotland and celebrate with us at short notice. Your father and I don't want to wait. We are hoping for a simple ceremony, as soon as possible. There's no point in dragging it out,' she finished. 'Do you agree?'

Jenny nodded. 'I agree. But it's sad that your family won't be with you.'

'Well . . .' Ellen looked thoughtful. 'Perhaps, later in the year, Fraser and I will go and visit them in Canada. That would be fun.'

'And me too?' Jenny teased.

Ellen laughed and ruffled Jenny's hair. 'We'll see. Is David still asleep?'

'I haven't seen him this morning,' Jenny replied. 'So he must be snoozing.'

'Your dad has asked for a cooked break—' Mrs Grace broke off as the phone rang.

'I'll get it!' Jenny said, sprinting into the hall. 'Hello?'

'It's me, Jen,' Carrie's voice sounded faint, as though she was phoning from a long way away.

'Carrie! I was just thinking about you and hoping you might feel like a walk with Jess and . . .'

'I'm going in to hospital – now,' she said flatly.

'Now? You mean, today?' Jenny was confused.

Ellen Grace had come into the hall, wiping her hands on a dish towel. 'What is it?' she whispered, alarmed by the look on Jenny's face.

'I just phoned to say goodbye,' Carrie said.

'But . . . why?' Jenny asked. 'Why do you have to go so suddenly?'

'I've come out in some little blood blisters, under my skin, which isn't a good sign. So I've got to go right away. Will you come and visit me?'

Jenny felt a wave of fear rising up from her feet and her mouth went dry. Mrs Grace put out a hand and Jenny clutched it.

'Yes, of course,' she said brightly. 'I'll be there. I'll bring some sweets . . .'

'The ambulance is here. I've got to go now. Bye, Jen.' The line went dead.

Jenny replaced the receiver and let go of Mrs Grace's hand. Jess was at her side in a trice, sitting as close to her as he could, pushing his nose into her palm.

'Tell me, Jenny!' Mrs Grace urged. 'What's happened?'

'An ambulance!' Jenny repeated, as if in a trance. 'Carrie's being taken to hospital.'

Ellen Grace wound her arms round Jenny and held her close. Then she guided her towards the big pine table and sat her down into a chair. She poured some hot tea from the big brown pot and stirred in two heaped spoonfuls of sugar.

'Take a sip,' she urged Jenny.

'Oh, Mrs Grace!' Jenny wailed, putting her head in her hands. 'Will I ever see Carrie again?'

'Of course you will,' Ellen Grace was firm. 'She's just having her operation a little sooner the planned, that's all. And didn't you just say that you'd visit her in the hospital?'

Jenny sipped at her hot tea, holding tightly to Mrs Grace's hand. Jess put his head into her lap, which

Jenny found comforting, as ever. She took a deep breath. She would have to try hard not to be afraid for Carrie, but to believe, as she always had, that she was going to get well.

'Brave girl!' said Ellen Grace gently, as Jenny managed a watery smile.

When Matt and Fraser Miles had gone off into the fields, and David had gone upstairs to do his homework, Jenny decided to head off up to Darktarn Keep. It was the one place where she could be alone with her thoughts, her own special place to be when there were things she wanted to come to terms with.

Jess's tail thumped steadily against the floor of the kitchen, watching as she fastened Orla's lead onto her collar. She pulled on a fleece and her boots, while Orla yapped steadily in excitement. Then, the kitchen door open, Orla raced out into the yard after Jess, dragging Jenny along behind her.

As soon as she reached the track that ran up the hill, Jenny let Orla off her lead. The dogs bounded on ahead, up the steep rise that led to the stone keep on its crest. A sharp wind rose from a choppy, grey sea far below, but Jenny knew that when she reached the protective shelter of Darktarn's thick and ancient stone walls, she would be snug in the spring sunshine.

THE GIFT

It was hard to look down on the cluster of colourful houses in Cliffbay and know that Carrie wasn't there, where she should be. Somewhere over in Greybridge, her friend was lying on a starched white hospital sheet, in a room smelling of disinfectant, and she, Jenny, hadn't even been there to give her a goodbye hug. It wasn't the way she had imagined it at all.

'Blisters?' Mr Miles had said at breakfast time, befuddled from a late sleep and concerned by his daughter's pale and anxious face. 'Doesn't sound very serious to me, Jen.' He and Matt, and David too, had comforted and reassured her, but Jenny's fear lay like a cold and heavy stone in the pit of her tummy – and it refused to budge.

Jess bounded up to the place where Jenny was sitting, her back to the wall, in a pool of soft sunshine. He curled up beside her, lifting his head to look at the gulls that circled lazily above the cliff top on wide, white wings. Together they watched Orla, as she wandered about on the hillside, seeking out and following the scent of fox and rabbit.

'Oh, Jess,' Jenny said quietly. 'What will I do if Carrie dies?' Jess licked Jenny's hand and looked up at her with his intense, caramel-coloured eyes. Then, he stood up and wagged his tail. 'You're right,' she said, smiling at him. 'I'm being far too gloomy. I must try not to think about it. *Especially* when there is a wedding to plan!'

Even the thought of Ellen Grace was somehow comforting. 'I do love her, Jess,' she told him. 'Not in the same way that I loved Mum, but it's love nevertheless. I'm sure of it now. And Mum would be pleased to know there was someone taking care of us at Windy Hill. Don't you think? What am I going to get them as a present, I wonder?'

Jess put his paw into her lap and Jenny was idly examining the little black pad for signs of the wound made by the splinter, when she felt the collie stiffen. Someone was walking slowly up the hill. Jess's ears were alert and he watched intently as the figure approached. Then his ears went down and he streaked away towards it, his tail streaming out behind him.

Jenny soon recognised Mrs Turner. She was carrying an easel and had her painting things in a leather case over her shoulder. Jenny had seen these tools before and was encouraged by the sight of them. If Mrs Turner was here to paint, it must mean there was good news about Carrie. She jumped up and ran to meet her.

'Mrs Turner!' Jenny called. Carrie's mum turned, frowning, and Jenny saw immediately that she had been crying. Her red eyes were ringed with the dark smudges of sleeplessness. Jenny's heart felt as though it had jumped into her throat. 'How's Carrie?'

'Hello, Jenny,' Mrs Turner said quietly. She began to set up her easel. Away in the distance, Orla yapped and pounced on something, but Jess stayed beside Jenny. 'There's no news, just yet,' she said.

'But . . . the hospital . . . what happened?' Jenny pleaded. Her voice was almost a whisper.

'Carrie's condition suddenly got worse,' she explained. 'She's getting tiny blood blisters under her skin which means that her blood isn't clotting properly. The doctors say that's bad sign because the bone marrow is breaking down very quickly, and Carrie is without an effective immune system.'

Jenny slowly shook her head, then looked out towards the sea. She didn't want Mrs Turner to see her cry. 'But Sarah Taylor is going to help . . .'

'Yes,' Mrs Turner brushed her red hair away from her face and straightened her shoulders. She took a deep breath. 'Yes, I'm sure that will give Carrie the chance she needs to get better.'

'When will she be able to come home?' Jenny asked.

'We don't know yet,' Mrs Turner replied. She unrolled a large canvas and set it up on the easel. 'I'm going back to the hospital later. In the meantime, painting will help me to relax.'

'Yes,' Jenny agreed.

'There isn't really much I can do at the moment and Carrie's father and I both feel that our worrying and fussing will only make Carrie feel upset. Her dad's at home cooking a meal – it's his way of relaxing.' She squeezed out a blob of green paint.

Jenny realised that she was looking at a picture that was almost complete. It showed the rugged, wild-flower strewn fields stretching down to the cliffs below Graston, and beyond, to a glassy grey sea. The red rooftops of Windy Hill had been painted in the foreground, standing out in sharp contrast to the hazy gold background of setting sun and sky. It was a lovely picture and, for a moment, Jenny wondered if she might ask Mrs Turner to paint her one just like it, as a gift for Mrs Grace and her father. Then she dismissed the idea as being foolish. Mrs Turner had more important things to think about.

'Are you walking Orla for David?' Mrs Turner asked.

'Yes. David's doing his homework,' Jenny explained. 'Orla loves coming with me and Jess. But I haven't really been walking. I've been sitting in the keep and thinking.'

'About Carrie?' Mrs Turner was daubing colour into a tiny gull's wing on her painting.

'Yes, and also about my dad – and Mrs Grace.'

'Yes?' Mrs Turner smiled at Jenny. 'And what *were* you thinking about them?' she prompted, a sparkle in her eye.

'Well,' Jenny began, 'Did you know they're getting married?'

'I suspected they might!' Carrie's mum laughed and for a moment her face was the way Jenny remembered it being before Carrie got sick. 'How wonderful. Are you pleased?'

'Yes,' Jenny nodded, certain of it now. She paused. 'I was wondering what I'd give them as a present. I haven't got a lot of pocket money left and . . .'

'But . . . you must have this *painting*!' Mrs Turner said, putting her hands on Jenny's shoulders and reading her thoughts.

'Oh Mrs Turner! Would you let me buy it?' Jenny was thrilled.

'Buy it! Nonsense, Jenny. You can have it to give to them – with my love!' she said.

'Really? It would be perfect for them. Dad has a very old aerial photograph of the farm, but nothing like this. They'll love it.' Jenny's eyes were shining.

'I expect there are a lot of plans to be made, now.'

Mrs Turner went back to her easel.

'Yes,' Jenny replied. 'It's hard for me to think about a wedding when Carrie . . .'

'Oh, but you must,' Mrs Turner said resolutely. 'Concentrate on your father's happiness — be as involved as you can. It will help the time to pass.' Mrs Turner's troubled eyes filled with tears.

'Thanks so much for the painting. It's really great,' Jenny said quietly.

'We'll keep it our secret, until it's finished. Then I'll wrap it for you,' she said.

Jenny nodded, smiling. 'I'd better get back,' she said.

'Bye, Jenny.' Mrs Turner was already painting again. But suddenly she turned to get up and give Jenny a hug. 'You're a good friend to Carrie,' she murmured in her ear. 'The best.'

9

On the way back down the track to Windy Hill, Jenny tried hard not to think about Carrie but of the coming wedding instead. Mrs Turner was right; there was little point in dwelling on the sad and frightening possibilities of her friend's sickness. She tried to picture the dress Ellen might choose to wear on her special day, and wondered whether there would be a party, and how thrilled her dad would be with Carrie's mum's painting.

Jenny called to Orla. The collie had spotted a rabbit

and raced after it. She was sprinting in sweeping circles across the field below. Jess showed no interest in joining her. He kept close to his mistress's side, his icy nose never far from her hand, his tail drooping.

'I'm OK,' Jenny told him, her fingers on his silky head. 'Don't you worry, Jess. I'll be fine. I'm not the one who's sick.'

Orla arrived, panting heavily from her run, and Jenny fastened her lead onto her collar as they reached the boundary of the farm. Fraser Miles had warned both David and Jenny not to allow Orla to roam anywhere near his sheep, and it was a precaution Jenny had taken to heart.

When she reached the farmyard, she recognised Mr Fergusson's car on the gravel forecourt. The front door of the farmhouse opened and David stepped out, his sports bag in his hand. Jenny could tell it had been packed in a hurry, because the zip hadn't properly closed and she could see the trailing sleeve of a grey school jumper.

'Dad's home,' David said, as Jenny approached. 'Thanks for walking Orla.' Jess and Orla greeted David with wagging tails.

'Are you leaving?' she asked.

'Yeh. He just arrived back. Mrs Grace told me Carrie's been taken to hospital.' David's dark eyebrows were high on his forehead.

Jenny nodded. 'Poor Carrie. She suddenly got worse.'

'Hello, Jenny,' said Mr Fergusson, stepping out of the house with Mr Miles. Jenny's father was in his wellington boots. Nell and Jake milled around his legs, obviously eager to get back to work.

'Hello, Mr Fergusson.'

'Thanks for having my boy,' he smiled.

Jenny wondered again why this man seemed so mysterious; why hadn't he telephoned to say he was on his way back? And why hadn't he been able to tell them how long he would be gone in the first place?

'Yes, thanks,' David nodded at Mr Miles. 'Thanks for letting me stay, Mr Miles.'

'It was nice to have you around,' said Jenny's dad.

Mr Fergusson threw David's bag into the back of the car and Orla jumped in after it. Jess went to the car and looked up. Orla's head appeared over the sill of the back window and the collie's touched noses, briefly.

'Ah,' said Jenny. 'They're saying goodbye.'

'See you at school tomorrow,' David said, getting in.

'Yes. Bye.'

As David's father drove away, Jenny felt a small pang

of regret. She was going to miss having David around.

'*Ellen!*' said Jenny, trying the name out as she came into the kitchen.

Mrs Grace turned, and gave Jenny a happy smile. 'Oh, that *does* sound . . . friendly!' She laughed, and put her arm round Jenny's shoulders. 'It makes me feel that I'm really part of the family!'

'Good,' said Jenny, smiling inwardly about the wonderful secret of Mrs Turner's painting. 'I saw Mrs Turner up near Darktarn Keep. She had been crying,' Jenny reported, her face suddenly serious.

'Did she explain what had caused Carrie to be taken in to hospital like that?' Ellen asked.

'Something about how the cells that clot Carrie's blood weren't working properly any more,' Jenny said, not really wanting to think about it. She changed the subject. 'Mrs Grace . . . Ellen, are you going to wear a white dress for the wedding?'

'Good heavens, no!' Ellen laughed. 'I'm too old for all that. No, something rather glamorous, but dignified, I think. Will you help me choose something?'

'Yes, please!' Jenny eyes lit up.

'And perhaps you'd like to have something special to wear yourself?' Ellen asked.

'Wow, yes!' It had been ages since Jenny had been shopping for clothes.

'Your father and I would like it to be a small wedding. We don't want a big fuss. But there is lots to be done, just the same. Do you want to help me to plan it?' Ellen Grace asked.

Jess barked, and Jenny laughed. 'He approves!' she said. 'And so do I! Yes, when do we start – and where?'

'We'll start with a list of people,' Ellen said. 'Have you got a pen?'

'I'll just fill Jess's water bowl,' Jenny said, 'and then I'll be with you.' It wasn't very long ago, Jenny reflected, that she was making out a list for a different sort of party. Still, it was good to be busy. It was just what she needed.

After lunch, Matt announced that he would have to make an early start back to college. 'There's a party on tonight in my residence,' he said. 'I don't want to miss it.'

'You deserve it,' Fraser Miles grinned at his son. 'You've worked hard this weekend. Thanks, Matt.'

Jenny trailed after Matt as he hurried around his bedroom, packing. 'Are you feeling happier? About Dad and Mrs Grace, I mean?' she asked.

'I . . . think so,' Matt said thoughtfully. 'Ellen is lovely, isn't she? And you are right, Jen. Dad could have chosen to marry someone like that awful Marion woman!'

At the mention of her name, Jenny gave a shudder. 'Ugh! Don't remind me.'

'Jenny!' Ellen Grace's voice came floating up the stairs. 'Fiona's here. She's going to the hospital to visit Carrie. Do you want to go along?'

Jenny gasped. 'Yes!' she shouted. 'I'm coming!' She raced along the passage and took the stairs two at a time.

'Goodbye, Jenny!' Matt's voice was playfully sarcastic.

'Oh, sorry, Matt,' Jenny paused at the bottom of the stairs and yelled. 'Bye – see you next weekend.' Jess had been lying on the floor under the table, and now he got up and came over to Jenny, wagging his tail happily. She planted a kiss on the soft place between the collie's eyes. 'No, no walk just now. Stay there, boy. I won't be long.'

'Give Carrie our love,' Ellen Grace's hands were clasped at her chest.

'I'm so glad I can *see* her!' Jenny breathed, lacing up her trainers in a hurry. 'I didn't think I would. Not for ages. But I haven't got any *sweets*!'

'Don't worry about that. And don't expect too much, will you?' Ellen Grace looked anxious.

'I won't,' Jenny said. 'See you later.' And she sped out of the door just as Fiona leaned forward to toot the horn impatiently on her mother's car.

In the children's ward at Greybridge Hospital, Carrie had her own small room. On a coatstand in the corner, hung a series of snowy-white gowns which reminded Jenny of a ghost costume she'd once worn at Hallowe'en. There was a blue chalk-line marked on the floor around Carrie's bed, which she had to stay behind. Carrie lay inside a special little see-through tent, which had been filled with air that was being kept carefully germ-free.

Jenny stared at her friend. She looked so small and helpless on the other side of the plastic. Her face was several shades paler than when Jenny had last seen her, whirling about in a wild Scottish reel in her father's arms. A rash of tiny blood blisters marked her neck and her hands.

'I'm an alien,' said Carrie, lifting her pyjamas to show them a thin, soft tube emerging from a tiny hole in her tummy. She made a face, and Jenny found herself giggling, though it wasn't funny at all. Carrie's tummy had been painted with a bright orange liquid

to keep it sterile and it looked rather painful.

'It doesn't hurt,' she added, as Fiona's hands flew to cover her mouth in horror. 'They put all the medicine in through there, and take some of my blood out. And they'll put Sarah's marrow through there for me, too,' Carrie explained matter-of-factly. 'It's far better than having lots of injections!'

'Yes,' Jenny agreed. There seemed little point in asking Carrie how she was feeling. Jenny could guess that her friend was being brave, but watching her, Jenny felt her heart thud loudly in her chest.

'You didn't bring Jess?' Carrie joked.

'Not allowed,' Jenny grinned. 'He wanted to come, though.'

'What's the food like?' Fiona wanted to know. Jenny could tell she was uneasy.

'Quite good,' was Carrie's response. She shifted the cloth cap she was wearing on her head. The remaining wisps of her red hair were just visible. 'I'm not very hungry, though.'

'Are you scared?' Fiona asked, gazing around the room at all the monitoring equipment. 'Of the operation, I mean?'

'Nope,' said Carrie dismissively. 'I'll be asleep, and when I wake up, it'll all be over.'

The heavy white door of the hospital room swung

open and Sarah Taylor peeped round it. Mrs Turner and a doctor were with her. Behind them, Mrs MacLay was sipping a hot drink from a plastic cup.

'Hello!' Sarah smiled, coming in. She looked at Jenny and Fiona. 'Gosh, the whole gang's here!' She was wearing a green hospital gown and her hair had been scooped up inside a paper cap. There was a sticking-plaster on her arm.

Jenny and Fiona said hello, together.

'All right, Carrie?' asked the doctor, peering in on her. Carrie nodded.

'I'm just along the corridor from you, Carrie,' Sarah said.

'Sarah's going to have her bone marrow removed this afternoon,' the doctor announced. 'The operation will last about an hour, then she'll go into the recovery room. Then it'll be your turn.' He smiled warmly at Carrie, who blinked at him.

'It'll be over before you know it, Carrie lass,' Anna MacLay said reassuringly.

'How do they get it out? The marrow?' Fiona asked Sarah.

'They collect it from the bones of the pelvis – which is this bit here,' Sarah pointed to the area around her hips. 'They put in a special needle and draw out the marrow – only about one litre. I can go

home tomorrow, can't I, Doctor?' Sarah asked.

'You sure can,' he said cheerfully.

Fiona was grimacing. 'Ooh, it sounds painful!'

'A little bit,' said the doctor. 'But she'll be back at that wildlife hospital of hers in a few days.'

'What time will Carrie have her operation, Doctor Willis?' Mrs Turner asked in a small voice.

'About five o clock,' he replied.

Jenny felt as though she didn't want to hear any more about it. She wanted it to be over and for Carrie to be well again. She tried to concentrate on a picture of Carrie running along the path above Cliffbay, the wind whipping her tangled red hair away from her laughing face. It made her feel better. 'When will you be home again?' she asked, looking at Carrie, but directing the question at the doctor.

'That will depend on her white blood cell count,' the doctor explained. 'When it's back up to a healthy number of cells, which are fighting fit, she can go home. It shouldn't take more than about ten days to two weeks.'

'Oh,' said Jenny, and remembered to smile brightly at Carrie.

'May I have a word, Mrs Turner?' the doctor asked. Carrie's mum followed him out of the room.

Carrie yawned, and turned her head away on the

pillow. She looked so sad that Jenny's heart turned over.

'I think it's time we were off,' said Mrs MacLay quietly. 'Fiona? Jenny?'

'Yes,' Jenny said. She wished she could slip her hand into Carrie's sterile tent and squeeze her fingers, or crawl right under it and give her a hug. 'Good luck, Carrie,' she said simply.

'Bye, Carrie,' Fiona echoed.

'Say hello to Jess for me,' Carrie smiled at Jenny. She lifted her fingers in a limp little wave.

'Goodbye.' Jenny was glad to get out of the room. The tears that had been threatening since the start of their visit began to spill silently down her cheeks.

'It was *horrible!*' Jenny told Ellen Grace. She paced about the kitchen back at Windy Hill, unable to settle. Mrs Grace clasped a mug of tea and watched her sadly. In his basket Jess's ears were pricked, his head to one side, as he followed Jenny with eyes full of concern.

'Seeing her lying there, looking so . . . white and blotchy and sick. It was horrible,' she said again. Her tears had dried up, and in their place had come a fierce anger at the unfairness of it all.

'Well,' Ellen Grace spoke soothingly. 'It's all

117

happened sooner than we expected. But this is the first step to Carrie's recovery, Jenny. Try to think of it that way. The next time you see her, she may be just like the old, fiery redhead we know and love.'

Jenny stopped striding about, and drew up a chair beside Ellen. She put her chin in her hands. 'How am I going to stop thinking about it?' she asked. 'Until she's better?'

'For a start, we've got a wedding to plan,' Ellen Grace smiled. 'And there's that new dress you wanted . . .'

Jenny sat up and gave herself a little shake. 'Yes,' she

said. 'That's a nice thought. A new dress . . .'

'I've got a friend in Graston who is a wonderfully clever dressmaker,' Mrs Grace said. 'If you like, we could pop along and see her this evening . . . get some ideas?'

'I'd like that,' Jenny smiled. 'That will take my mind off Carrie.'

Jess wandered over to Jenny, looking forlorn. She could tell by his face and the expression in his eyes that he knew something was up. Jenny hadn't paid him the usual amount of attention. She realised now, with a stab of guilt – that she hadn't given his coat a good brushing for days.

Jenny slipped off her chair and sat down on the floor beside the collie. Jess rolled over onto his back, his tail wagging. His bright button eyes blinked happily at her. 'I want to give Jess a cuddle,' she told Ellen, 'and then I'll be ready to go!'

10

The morning of the wedding, two weeks later, dawned a murky grey. Light rain and a playful breeze quickly turned into a downpour, with wind that buffeted around the farmhouse and made the windows shake.

In her bedroom, Jenny was putting on the dress made for her by Ellen Grace's friend. She was examining herself in the mirror, watching the jade green of her silk skirt twirl about as she moved. The dress was beautiful, very simple in design, with a matching blue silk jacket. It had been carefully chosen to complement Ellen's. Jenny never usually gave a thought to her clothes – and she certainly wouldn't have chosen a fussy, full dress for the wedding, but even she was pleased with the way she looked.

At the thought of the ceremony to come, the butterflies in her tummy began to flutter. Sheena Miles, Jenny's mother, smiled serenely at her from the photograph frame on her desk, and she went over and planted a little kiss on it.

She hadn't thought of her dad as being lonely before. After all, he had his blackfaces and his beloved Windy Hill, and a daughter who loved him . . . but the look on his face, ever since Ellen Grace had accepted the pretty, antique pearl ring he had given her, told a different story.

Jenny went over to the window and looked out over the rain-soaked fields of the farm. She willed the rain to stop and the sun to come out, for Ellen and her father's walk down the aisle of the church. A sunny day seemed right, somehow. Lifting the frill of her bedcover, she peered under the bed. Mrs Turner's painting was there, lying flat, wrapped in a single cotton sheet and tied with string like a parcel. Carrie's mum had added more detail to the canvas, putting in the shearing shed that stood at right angles to the house, the stable block and the lambing barn. 'To make it more personal,' she had said. The painting was the perfect gift.

Jenny brushed her hair, and twisted it into a neat little knot on the top of her head, the way Ellen had shown her. She looked again at the picture of her mother, then opened her bedroom door.

'Well!' breathed Matt, when she appeared in the kitchen. 'Who would have thought they could make a *lady* out of you!' He grinned at his sister as Jess hurried over, wagging his tail.

'I hope we can make a best man out of *you*,' she retorted, teasingly, patting the collie. 'Look at the state of you!' Matt's hair was standing up in peaks, and his face and clothes were dirty.

'I'll have you know I was up half the night with one of our ewes,' Matt said, rubbing his eyes. 'Nasty case of foot rot. Anyway I've got time to shower and spruce myself up.'

'I hope so,' Jenny smiled. 'How's the ewe now?'

'Better. Dozing peacefully last time I checked. Nell wouldn't leave her though. She's lying up there in the barn with her.'

'How sweet,' said Jenny. 'Do you like my dress?' She spun around, showing it off.

'I haven't ever seen you look so good,' Matt said seriously.

'Are you happy – about Dad and Ellen, I mean?' Jenny checked again.

'Dad's is over the moon, isn't he? Then it must be right.' Matt yawned and stretched. 'Well, I'd better go and get ready.'

'Oh, Matt, before you go, can I have a peep at the rings?'

'All right.' He stood up. 'They're over here, in this dresser drawer . . . no . . . wait a minute!' Matt frowned and put his hands on his hips.

Jenny had to stand on tiptoe to see inside the small top drawer of the dresser. It was empty. 'Oh! Matt,' she said in dismay. 'You haven't lost them!'

'Now, don't panic. I'm sure I've put them somewhere sensible. Let's think . . .'

'Yesterday morning – you picked them up for Dad from the jeweller in Greybridge. Did you leave them in the car?'

'I couldn't have! But I'll go and check.' Matt dashed to the kitchen door and flung it open. 'Ugh!' he shouted, as a shower of rain blew into his face.

'You're not going for a walk in this weather are you, Matt?' Ellen Grace stepped into the room. Matt had vanished round the side of the house. 'Jenny . . .

where *is* your brother go— Oh! Jenny, you look perfect, love.'

'Thanks.' Jenny looked down at the dress she wore.

The kitchen door slammed shut and Matt reappeared, looking more dishevelled than ever. 'I can't understand it!' he said, perplexed. 'I'm usually so practical . . .'

'So careless, more like!' Jenny said crossly.

'What's happened?' Ellen asked.

'Matt's lost the rings.' Jenny said flatly.

'I've misplaced them, that's all,' Matt said.

'Oh!' Ellen's face fell. She looked around the kitchen, rather helplessly. 'But where . . . oh! what on *earth* is Jess up to?'

The collie was in the small utility room to the side of the kitchen. Through the open door they could see him burrowing frantically in the laundry basket. He had managed to overturn it and, with his scrabbling paws, was dragging out the items of dirty clothing waiting to be washed.

'Jess!' Matt bellowed, his irritation rising.

'Wait,' said Jenny. 'Jess never does anything without a good reason. Did you, by any chance, put the rings into a pocket? Jeans? Trousers? Jacket?'

Jess had singled out a pair of corduroy trousers. He grabbed hold of the fabric with his teeth and began to shake them, as Jenny had seen hunting dogs do with wild animals.

Matt's face broke into a smile. 'Yes! You're right, Jess! Well done, boy!' He patted the collie's side and took the trousers from him. Slipping his hand into the pocket, he pulled out a small, navy-blue box. 'Here they are!' Matt was triumphant, while Jenny ruffled Jess's ears.

'Good boy!' Jenny turned to her brother. 'You'd better go and get washed and changed!' Matt saluted her mockingly, and hurried off up the stairs, as Jenny remembered she still hadn't had a look at the rings.

'Jess!' laughed Ellen. 'You're a hero.'

There was a knock at the door. Jenny ran to open it.

Mrs Turner was standing dripping in the porch, holding a small bouquet of flowers. 'Oh! Don't you look lovely, Jenny!' she smiled.

Jenny smiled back at her, then stepped aside quickly to let her in as she hid the flowers behind her back.

'I know you said you thought carrying a bouquet might be overdoing it,' Mrs Turner said to Ellen Grace, 'but I thought something small and pretty might be suitable.'

Ellen Grace drew in her breath as Mrs Turner held

out a bunch of delicate lilac and white flowers, tied with a wide white satin ribbon. 'They're lovely! Thank you so much.'

'They'll look perfect with your dress too!' Jenny said, admiring Mrs Turner's artistic touch. Then she added: 'How's Carrie?'

'She was much brighter when I saw her last night,' Mrs Turner said. 'The transplant seems to have been a success. Of course, she's desperate to get out of the hospital and is giving everyone there a hard time. But it won't be long now, because her white blood count is rising steadily.'

'What good news,' said Ellen, putting the stems of her flowers into a jug of water.

Jenny was disappointed. She had badly wanted Carrie to see the ceremony. She had been in hospital a full two weeks and Jenny had expected her friend to be better by now. She bent to smooth Jess's head so Mrs Turner wouldn't notice her disappointment.

The collie's tail went from side to side. Jenny knew that he could sense the excitement in the room. Now, his ears pricked up and he ran to the back door and barked happily. There was a loud knocking.

'It's like Edinburgh station in here this morning,' laughed Ellen. 'At rush hour!'

'David!' said Jenny, as she opened the door. 'Come in . . .'

But David had already pushed past her and into the kitchen. He appeared not to notice her dress. Jenny saw Ellen Grace glance down at his feet, which were mud-covered. The rain dripped off him, forming a small puddle on the kitchen floor. Droplets of rain were scattered across his dark hair and sparkled there like jewels.

'Hello, David,' Ellen and Mrs Turner said together.

'I know it's the day of your wedding and everything but I had to come! There's some news . . . you see, I think, that is, *we* think . . .' David was speaking so fast he couldn't get the words out. Jenny had never seen him so excited.

'Hang on,' Jenny laughed. 'Take it slowly! We? We who?'

'My dad and I,' David said, checking himself. He took a deep breath. 'We think that Jess is the father!'

'What?' Jenny asked, frowning. She was instantly protective and her hand went out to the collie. 'What do you mean?'

'Orla is going to be a mum!' David finished, his eyes shining. 'You see, we noticed she was putting on weight. She seemed so hungry; so Dad said we should take her to the vet. Mr Palmer said there's nothing wrong with her at all, only, she's going to have puppies!'

'Oh, Ellen! Can it be true?' Jenny thought she was going to burst with excitement.

'I don't see why not. After all, Jess and Orla were together here at Windy Hill for quite a while.' Ellen Grace was smiling.

Jenny let out a little shriek of excitment. 'We're going to be . . . parents!' she shouted and David burst into laughter.

'What *do* you mean?' Matt asked. He was combing his wet hair with one hand as he walked, and brushing the lapel of his dark suit with the other. Jess began to bark and dance about. 'Has everyone gone completely mad?'

'I'll leave you now,' Mrs Turner chuckled, 'and see you later at the church.'

'Oops, sorry about the mess,' David said, looking down at the floor.

'I don't mind. It'll mop up,' Ellen Grace sighed. 'As long as nobody goes into the front room where the reception will be. It's been polished and prepared to perfection!'

'Matt!' Jenny tugged the sleeve of his suit. 'Jess is going to be a father! Orla's going to have puppies!'

'Hey, that's great,' Matt grinned.

Jenny turned to David, her face serious. 'David,' she breathed, 'you won't want to keep all of the pups, will you? I mean, you'll want to find homes for some, won't you?'

'I don't know if my dad will let me keep any of them,' David shook his head.

'Carrie would love one!' Jenny decided impulsively. 'And so would I! Can I? Have one for Carrie and one for me, I mean?'

'I don't see why not,' David said. 'We'll have to see how many are born, though.'

'Well, that's wonderful news, David,' Mrs Grace said. 'Thank you for coming to tell us. I must go and get changed now, or Fraser will be at the altar wondering if I've changed my mind!'

Matt looked at his watch. 'I'm off to collect Dad at Dunraven now,' he said. He walked over and gave Ellen a kiss on her cheek. 'We'll see you in church, Ellen.'

To Jenny's relief, the cloud began to break up just before they left Windy Hill for the church. When the convoy of cars reached St Thomas's, the fourteenth-century chapel on the outskirts of Graston, the spring sun was beaming down on its ancient slate roof.

Steam was rising from the grass in spirals like smoke. The wind had blasted the flimsy blossom from a cherry tree in the churchyard, and the petals lay along the stone path as though someone had scattered fragrant, pink confetti.

Jenny patted her hair into place and took a deep breath. Everything was ready, and it was going to be a wonderful day. She thought of the party to come back to Windy Hill. The dining-room table had been draped with a snowy cloth; and she knew that her father had borrowed a silver bucket to chill a special bottle of champagne. Matt had helped her to sneak Mrs Turner's painting down to the sitting-room, and it was now propped against the sofa, a surprise, waiting to be unwrapped. Jenny could hardly wait to see her father and Ellen's faces when they first saw it. She smiled to herself as Matt parked the car. The only thing spoiling her complete happiness today was that Carrie wasn't with her.

'You look absolutely wonderful,' she whispered to Ellen, as she got out of the car.

Mrs Grace wore a suit of the palest oyster grey and a frothy, cream-coloured hat. 'Thank you,' she smiled. 'I feel wonderful – except I'm afraid this hat looks a little bit like a meringue!'

Jenny spotted Fiona with her parents, Anna and

Callum MacLay, standing in a group of people outside the church. There was Paul, and Mr Turner and Tom Palmer and his wife, and several of the farmers in the district whom her father knew, and Mr Fergusson with David. Jenny recognised many of the faces from having seen them in the village hall, at Carrie's surprise party. Just then, Father Finn arrived, and the crowd followed him into the chapel.

Jess stood proudly beside Jenny. She believed that he knew that it was a very special occasion and she trusted that he would be on his best behaviour. The collie's head was high, his tail was still, all of his boundless energy curbed for this important occasion.

'Mum would have loved you,' Jenny whispered, and reminded herself to bring up the subject of keeping one of Jess's puppies with her father after the ceremony.

She walked with Jess, behind Ellen, into the dim, cool interior, as the organ music rang out and the guests inside got to their feet.

As Jenny went slowly down the aisle towards her father and brother, her eyes swivelled from side to side, hoping, by some miracle, that Carrie would be there on this special day. Sarah Taylor smiled at her and Mr Turner grinned and waved. Jenny couldn't see Mrs Turner anywhere in the church and she wondered if she had decided to visit Carrie in hospital instead.

Fraser Miles, wearing a crisp, charcoal-grey suit, glanced behind him to smile encouragingly at Ellen as she came to join him at the altar. Jenny noticed her brother nudge him gently with his elbow and wink. She and Ellen reached them, and Father Finn's deep voice began to ring out, echoing around the tiny church as he began the ceremony.

Jenny saw Ellen glance up at her father. Her face was radiant; she blinked back tears of joy. She held Mrs Turner's bouquet in one hand, the satin ribbon trailing down the front of her elegant dress, and with the other she nervously clutched one of Fraser Miles's big hands.

Father Finn paused to open his Bible – and there was a shuffling disturbance from the back of the church. Jenny felt Jess's tail began to twitch, then he wagged it hard against her. Jenny put a restraining hand on his head and looked behind her.

The old wooden door had been pushed open, and someone at the back had jumped up to hold it there. Mrs Turner, her scarlet hat askew, was steering a small wheelchair into the chapel. Wearing a baseball cap for the occasion, Carrie smiled out at the sea of faces staring back at her.

'Sorry we're late,' she said, her voice echoing and loud in the sudden silence.

Jenny gasped with delight and only just stopped herself from rushing to the back of the church to fling her arms around her friend. Carrie, so small and pale in her chair, grinned at the crowd, bravely acknowledging their smiles of greeting.

Father Finn nodded, then went calmly back to his Bible, simply saying, 'A warm welcome to our courageous Carrie.'

Jenny listened solemnly, as her father and Mrs Grace became man and wife. Matt produced the rings at the right moment and Jess stood obediently all the way through the service. Once or twice, Jenny turned and caught Carrie's eye and smiled, and her heart gave a little jump with happiness.

She had a new mother; Jess was going to be a father of a whole litter of gorgeous pups – and it looked as though Carrie was going to beat her illness after all. Jenny wondered if she had ever felt happier.

'I wanted to surprise you,' Carrie said, when they were gathered outside the church after the service.

'I'm so glad you came,' said Jenny.

'We only just made it,' Mrs Turner explained. 'The doctor wasn't happy at all about Carrie leaving the hospital. But she made his life a misery until he agreed!'

'You mean . . .' Jenny said, 'that you have to go *back*? You're not finished with that place?'

'Not yet,' Carrie shook her head, and looked at her hands in her lap. 'Soon, maybe.'

'Oh.' Jenny struggled to mask her disappointment. 'I'll come and visit you,' she said cheerfully.

'Yes, of course you will,' said Carrie's mum briskly. 'Now, we really must be getting you back to Greybridge, Carrie, love.'

Fraser Miles and Ellen, Sarah, Fiona and Matt, crowded around Carrie's wheelchair to say their farewells. Jenny slipped her hand into Carrie's and gave it a squeeze. It was then that Jess nosed his way through to Carrie. Gently, he laid his head in her lap. He looked up at her, his chin on her knee.

'Ah, Jess,' Carrie murmured, stroking his head.

Jenny bent down and spoke softly in Carrie's ear. 'Guess what? Jess is going to be a dad! Orla is going to have puppies!'

Carrie's eyes were shining as she looked up at Jenny. 'Really? A whole lot of miniature Jesses running around. What a lovely thought!'

'David says he doesn't think his father will let him keep the puppies and so . . .'

'Goodbye, everyone, and thanks,' Mrs Turner interrupted. She sounded rather anxious, as she began to push Carrie's wheelchair.

Jenny stepped back. 'Bye. Thanks for coming.'

Fraser Miles offered his arm to his new bride as they went into the farmhouse at Windy Hill. Jenny hurried behind in them, so she could be there when they spotted the painting.

Ellen went into the sitting-room to make sure everything was ready for the party. 'What's this, Fraser?' she asked, pointing.

'It's my present, to you,' Jenny spoke up. 'I was hoping you would have time to open it before the guests get here.'

'Oh, Jenny!' Ellen was touched. 'How did you manage to keep *this* a secret? She and Jenny's father tugged at the string and the sheet fell away from the large rectangular canvas and sighed to the floor in a heap.

For a moment, nobody spoke. Then Ellen Miles covered her mouth with her fingers and tears sprang to her eyes. 'A painting! A painting of Windy Hill – I can't think of anything I would want more. Mrs Turner?' she asked Jenny.

Jenny nodded proudly.

'She's so talented – she's captured it all so well.' Ellen was glowing.

Fraser Miles put his arms round Jenny and hugged her. 'How many years have I dreamed of hanging a painting like this in this house? You're a marvel, my lass! Thank you.'

'Yes, thank you, Jenny,' Ellen said, dabbing at her eyes with a tissue.

Jenny was lost in a dreamy kind of happiness, admiring the beautiful painting, when the telephone rang.

'Get that, Jen, will you?' Matt yelled from the

kitchen. 'My hands are full of glasses and there are guests coming up the driveway.'

'Hello? Jenny Miles speaking.'

'It's me,' said Carrie.

'Carrie! Are you at Cliff House?' Jenny asked, confused.

'No, silly. I'm phoning from the hospital. It's about the puppies. Mum says you can put my name down for one of them, for when they're born, OK?'

'Wow! That's fantastic. You're going to be a pet owner, like me. We can go for long walks with the dogs together and . . .'

'I've got to go now,' Carrie interrupted. 'Don't forget, will you? I want a boy puppy, just like Jess.' The phone went dead.

Jenny replaced the receiver.

Jess, who was sitting beside Jenny, barked. She sat down on the floor and put her arms round his neck. Jess rested his head on her shoulder.

'You know,' said Jenny to the collie, 'I've got an awful lot to look forward to.'

ORDER FORM

Lucy Daniels

All Hodder Children's books are available at your local bookshop, or can be ordered direct from the publisher. Just tick the titles you would like and complete the details below. Prices and availability are subject to change without prior notice.

Please enclose a cheque or postal order made payable to *Bookpoint Ltd*, and send to: Hodder Children's Books, 39 Milton Park, Abingdon, OXON OX14 4TD, UK.
Email Address: orders@bookpoint.co.uk

If you would prefer to pay by credit card, our call centre team would be delighted to take your order by telephone. Our direct line *01235 400414* (lines open 9.00 am–6.00 pm Monday to Saturday, 24 hour message answering service). Alternatively you can send a fax on *01235 400454.*

TITLE		FIRST NAME		SURNAME	

ADDRESS
DAYTIME TEL: POST CODE

If you would prefer to pay by credit card, please complete:
Please debit my Visa/Access/Diner's Card/American Express (delete as applicable) card no:

Signature .... Expiry Date: ....

If you would NOT like to receive further information on our products please tick the box. ❐